ESCAPE FROM THE TOWER OF LONDON

THE RAVENMASTER'S SECRET

ELVIRA WOODRUFF

SCHOLASTIC PRESS
NEW YORK

Woodruff, Elvira. The Ravenmaster's Secret / by Elvira Woodruff. p. cm.
Summary: The eleven-year-old son of the Ravenmaster at the Tower of London
befriends a Jacobite rebel being held prisoner there.
ISBN 0-439-28133-4
1. Tower of London (London, England)—History—18th century—Juvenile fiction.
[1. Tower of London (London, England)—History—18th century—Fiction.
2. Jacobites—Fiction. 3. Ravens—Fiction. 4. Prisoners—Fiction. 5. London
(England)—History—18th century—Fiction.] I. Title. PZ7.W8606 Rav 2003
[Fic]—dc21   2002015963

10 9 8 7 6 5 4 3 2 1   03 04 05 06 07

Printed in the U.S.A.   23
First edition, November 2003
Map of the Tower of London by Jim McMahon © 2003 Scholastic, Inc.
Book design by Marijka Kostiw and Yvette Awad
The display type was set in Usher.
The text type was set in 13 pt. MrsEavesRoman.

The poem on page ix is from "The Prison Fortress" by Shelagh Abbott from
Great Escapes from the Tower of London by Yeoman Warder G. Abbott.
Reprinted by permission of Mr. G. Abbott.

With special thanks to Diane Nesin for her meticulous fact-checking of
the manuscript; to the extraordinarily generous people of HM Tower of
London, including Ravenmaster David Cope; Jeremy Ashbee, Assistant
Curator of Historic Buildings; and Chris Gidlow and Alison Heald of the
Curator's Department, for answering our many questions; and to Maggie
Stevaralgia from the Scholastic Library.

OTHER SCHOLASTIC PRESS BOOKS
BY ELVIRA WOODRUFF

NOVELS

The Christmas Doll

*The Orphan of Ellis Island:
A Time Travel Adventure*

The Magnificent Mummy Maker

George Washington's Socks

PICTURE BOOK

The Memory Coat
(illustrated by Michael Dooling)

FOR MY HUSBAND, JOE,

KEEPER OF MY HEART

AND REASON FOR MY SMILE . . .

— ELVIRA WOODRUFF PILYAR

. . . AND TO MY EDITOR,

DIANNE HESS,

WITH SPECIAL THANKS

Table of Contents

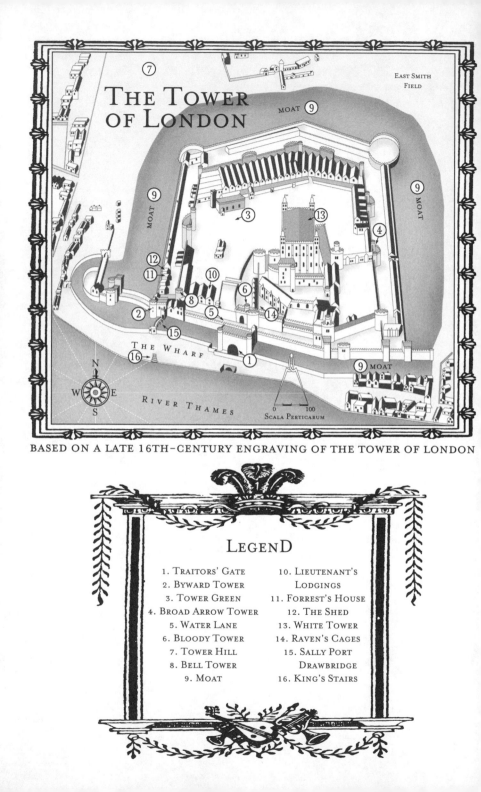

THE TOWER OF LONDON

BASED ON A LATE 16TH–CENTURY ENGRAVING OF THE TOWER OF LONDON

LEGEND

1. Traitors' Gate
2. Byward Tower
3. Tower Green
4. Broad Arrow Tower
5. Water Lane
6. Bloody Tower
7. Tower Hill
8. Bell Tower
9. Moat
10. Lieutenant's Lodgings
11. Forrest's House
12. The Shed
13. White Tower
14. Raven's Cages
15. Sally Port Drawbridge
16. King's Stairs

A BOX OF DRAUGHTS IS THIS THE TOWER OF LONDON.

A WHISTLING CAGE OF WEATHER

SET ON THE CITY'S EDGE.

BUT IF YOU WOULD FIND ONE CHINK, ONE SLIT

THROUGH WHICH A MAN MAY WEDGE HIS FINGER,

THEN YOU HAVE MAGIC, SIR, AND THERE'S AN END OF IT.

FOR STICK TO STONE

AS SKULL TO BONE,

TIGHT IS THIS PRISON BOUND.

AND CLEVER IS HE

WHO TO BE FREE

THINKS HE A PATH HATH FOUND. . . .

— FROM "THE PRISON FORTRESS"
BY SHELAGH ABBOTT

PROLOGUE:
WELCOME TO
THE TOWER OF LONDON

For more than nine hundred years the Tower of London has stood beside the River Thames. Over the centuries this massive, medieval fortress housed the Crown's jewels, the armory, the mint, and the zoo. But this ancient castle, with its many turrets, towers, battlements, and a moat, also held one of England's most notorious prisons. In times past, the very mention of its name filled people with dread.

The guards at the Tower were called Yeoman Warders, and they and their families were required to live within the fortress's high stone walls. In 1661, the royal astronomer to King Charles II complained that the wild ravens at the Tower were making too much racket and causing a nuisance. King Charles was about to have his archers destroy the birds, when he was reminded of the ancient legend that said if the ravens were ever to leave the Tower, it would fall to its enemies. The King then decreed that his archers should shoot all the birds, save nine. These remaining nine were to have their wings clipped so they could not fly away. They were to be provided with food and shelter within the Tower walls.

The job of caring for the magnificent black-winged creatures was given to one of the Yeoman Warders. Thus the position of Ravenmaster was created. Such a responsibility called for patience, steadfastness, and a keen eye, for the secrets of a raven's mind are not easily unraveled. To understand their ways, one must first gain their trust. This was no easy task, for ravens are naturally wary of men.

But there was one boy whom they trusted beyond all others, a boy whom they loved as much as he loved them, a boy who seemed born to the job. The year was 1735, the month was March, and the boy was Forrest Harper, son of Hugh Harper, Ravenmaster at the Tower of London.

I
WHAT NONSENSE
ARE YOU UP TO NOW?

"Chores, chores, and more chores," Forrest complained, as he threw the contents of his family's chamber pot over the moat wall.

"How am I ever to prove my courage, Tuck, if I am made to do nothing but chores all day?"

The raven on his shoulder gurgled in reply. The black ruff of his neck feathers glistened with mist as the rumble of a cart over a drawbridge sounded through the fog. Forrest frowned and gave the bottom of the pot a few good whacks with his fist to be sure it was empty. Tuck blinked into the wind that was blowing from the north.

If you happened to live beside one of the foulest smelling moats in all of Europe, your respect for the wind would be of no small measure. Standing beside this very moat, tucked into the Tower of London's outer walls, was a line of little cottages. It was here that the Tower's guards, or Yeoman Warders, lived with their wives and children. It was here that the Raven-master's son, eleven-year-old Forrest Harper, grew up.

Forrest was a boy who knew all about castle life. Since he was a small child, he played in the shadow of the Tower. He ran over drawbridges and under port-cullises. He floated leaf boats on the moat, dropped stones into murder holes, and peeked through arrow slits. But it was life outside the castle that he longed to experience. For he was sure that it was only in the out-side world that he could prove his courage.

He wrinkled his nose now, as the breeze picked up. The powerful stench at the Tower could be traced to one source. For hundreds of years every chamber pot in and around the fortress was emptied into its moat. All that raw sewage made for a mighty stink. But it was more than the evil-smelling air that caused Forrest to long for a change.

"If only Father were a sailor," he whispered to his pet raven, Tuck, "and we could travel with him on one of his voyages. There's no telling what adventures we could have, and surely I could prove my courage then."

Forrest suddenly jumped back, away from the wall, and pulled out an old spyglass from the leather case that hung across his chest.

"Pirates on the starboard side!" he cried, looking

through the glass. "Draw your weapon, you water-logged wretch," he shouted, as Tuck squawked in alarm.

Forrest slid the spyglass back into its case and reached for the slingshot in his pocket. He searched the ground for a stone.

"Dare to attack a vessel of the Crown?" he cried, as he pulled the leather back on his slingshot and sent the stone sailing above the brown scum of the moat's surface.

The loud, satisfying splash of the rock hitting the thick ooze was enough to send him searching for another. Even though his mother had forbid it, slinging stones into the moat was something he couldn't resist.

Tuck flew off the wall to follow the stone and was caught by the spray of murky water. Forrest hooted with laughter.

"You must be faster than that," he scolded, as he dried Tuck's tail feathers with his sleeve.

Tuck looked away as Forrest cleaned him, but he loved the boy and trusted his gentle touch.

Forrest had inherited his way with animals from his father. He had also inherited his father's thick hair, which was black as a raven's. From his mother's side came his sharp wits and his small size, for he was a full head shorter than most boys his age.

But the spark in Forrest Harper's eye was of his own making, for it came from a strong curiosity about the world and from a lively imagination. It was a spark that neither of his parents knew quite what to make of.

Though Forrest was always imagining himself on some new adventure, he rarely got to leave the confines of the dark old fortress. His days were spent cleaning cages and feeding the ravens. For two years, he had to go up and down the Bloody Tower's many steps as he fetched food for old Bishop Stafford, his father's sole prisoner.

This was one task Forrest looked forward to, for the Bishop was a friendly man who liked to tell stories about life outside the Tower. The many sights and sounds and names and places that the old priest described all found their way into Forrest's daydreams. When the King finally had the Bishop hanged, Forrest felt as if he'd lost his best friend as well as his only window to the outside world.

Before the Bishop was taken out of the Tower, he gave Forrest an old spyglass in a leather case. It was Forrest's prized possession, and it hung from a leather strap across his chest. Forrest often lifted the glass to his eye and imagined the sights he could see in the distance. But moisture had gotten into the lens and turned it so cloudy, it was impossible to really see anything through it, so Forrest had to pretend.

When he wasn't imagining himself off in some far-away land, Forrest was busy caring for the Tower's ravens. Because his chores took up most of the day, Forrest spent more time in the company of birds than boys. From his father, he learned the ways of ravens and discovered just how smart and playful they could be. It seemed only natural that Forrest's first pet would be a wild raven he raised from a fledgling.

Though Tuck was the same blue-black coloring as the Royal ravens, he was smaller, and because he was wild, his wings were not clipped. He was free to fly where he wished, which was usually as close to Forrest as he could get.

"You are the best pet in the world," Forrest told him now.

Tuck blinked as if in agreement.

"If only you could speak, Tuck. Can you say your name? Say 'Tuck.' Say 'Tuck, Tuck, Tuck.'"

The raven fluffed his head feathers. Forrest frowned. "Father says if I wanted a talking bird, I should have taken in a starling for a pet, for they love to chatter. But I know you will speak when you are ready, won't you? In the meantime we shall just keep practicing. Say 'Tuck. Tuck. Tuck. Tuck.'"

But the little raven could only answer with a soft "*kmm . . . kmm.*"

"Oh, Tuck, how will you warn me when the enemy comes to attack?" he asked, turning to look down the length of the high battlement wall that wrapped around the castle's moat.

He pulled the spyglass from its case and held it to his eye. "I can see a mountain road. What's that I spy coming our way? Three highwaymen on horseback! One has put a pistol to Father's head, while the other reaches for our lockbox under the wagon seat."

Forrest slipped the glass back into its case and quickly grabbed the chamber pot by its handle. Then he reached for a long stick lying on the ground. Holding the pot like a shield and the stick like a sword, he charged forward.

"Halt there, you impudent rascal of a highwayman. Halt, I say!" he shouted, stabbing the air before Tuck. "Give over that box, you fiend, or you shall know the fury of my broadsword."

"Alack, a day, what nonsense are you up to now?" a deep voice suddenly bellowed. Forrest spun around to see the towering figure of his father standing behind him.

II
YOU KNOW HOW YOUR MOTHER
LOVES A HANGING

Ravenmaster Hugh Harper had been a warder at the Tower for more than twenty-five years. He was in charge of the Tower's ravens as well as the prisoners the Constable placed under his guard. He wore the impressive warder's dress of crimson coat, high velvet hat, and stiff white ruff around his neck. He had a great silver beard, curled by the mist of the Thames, and a forehead as craggy and furrowed as the walls that held the river back. His breath smelled of juniper ale, and his fingers reeked of Dutch tobacco. From the tone of his voice and the scowl on his face, Forrest knew instantly that his father was in a bad temper this morning.

"I . . . I was just coming, Father," Forrest said, hiding the stick behind his back.

"And so is Midsummer's Day," his father growled. "Eleven years and your head is still stuffed with nonsense and child's play. Why, when I was your age, I was given the work of a man of twenty, and I . . ."

Forrest stared at his boots as he listened to the familiar words for the hundredth time.

"I worked from sun up to sun down, day in and day out. . . ."

Forrest had heard this particular lecture so often he was sure he could repeat it in his sleep.

"Yes, Father. Sorry, Father," he replied, as he always did.

"But that's not what I've come to tell you," the Ravenmaster continued. "I've just had news. There were three Scottish Rebels captured at York."

Forrest's ears pricked up.

"One is to be under our watch in the Bloody Tower. This will be no weak old priest, Forrest," his father began.

Forrest winced at the mention of his dear friend.

"But rather we've got a dangerous Jacobite, probably taken in battle. So quit your foolish ways, and look sharp. They should be but a day's ride away."

Forrest knew that the Jacobites were Scottish Rebels and followers of James Stuart, who claimed to be the rightful King of England. He also knew that their aim was to see England's own King George off the throne so that they could put a Stuart in his place.

"With Scotland so close to our borders, we dare not let the Rebels gain strength," his father said now. "I shudder to think how many should die if London were to fall."

"The city? Taken over by Scots?" Forrest gasped.

"Aye, if they had their way." His father sighed. "They're that determined."

Forrest felt a shiver run down his back. "How big is he, Father? Have you heard?"

The Ravenmaster shrugged. "I'd wager he's no bigger than most men."

"Has he killed many Englishmen?" Forrest asked excitedly. "Has he fought many battles?"

"I've not been told. Most likely we'll learn more once the prisoners are delivered to the Tower," said his father. "In the meantime, mind your work. Have you cleaned the cages?"

"Aye."

"And fed the birds?"

"Aye."

"Well, hurry home," his father said, with a wave of his white-gloved hand. "Your mother is anxious for your return. Have you forgotten what day it is?"

Forrest scratched his head. He had risen early, before his parents. He had talked to no one but Tuck all morning.

"Why, the church bells will be muffled all over the city," his father told him. " 'Twill be a day that most of

London will turn out for. Your mother could speak of little else this morning. Near boiled away the tea, she was going on about it so."

Forrest thought hard. "Is it Mother's birthday?"

"Mercy, no!" His father's stern face softened into a smile. "Your mother is a well-liked woman, but the city has yet to celebrate her birthday. No, lad, 'tis a collar day."

Forrest knew that the "collar" his father spoke of was the noose around a prisoner's neck. A collar day meant a hanging day. And while Forrest hated to see prisoners hanged, excitement was everywhere as the austere Tower grounds took on a carnival-like atmosphere.

"A Highwayman of noble birth is to stretch the rope at Tower Hill," his father continued. "Your mother and the girls have been dressed and waiting near an hour. So hurry home, for you know how your mother loves a hanging."

Forrest knew that he would be expected to accompany his mother and two little sisters to the execution, since his father could not leave his work at the Tower.

Without another word, Forrest took off down the path, with Tuck flying above him, his broadsword in one hand and the chamber pot in the other.

"Collar day," he called up to Tuck. "That means a day with people from the city, and music, and sweet tarts, and ginger beer! And jugglers, too!" But his smile suddenly faded.

"If only they did not have to hang people," he whispered. "Today could be the very best day of the year."

Tuck threw back his head and replied with a high-toned, "*Kek-kek-kek.*"

What neither boy nor bird could know then was that far from the best, this day would prove to be one of the very worst days of Forrest Harper's life. And it was all because of a Highwayman who was about to be hanged.

III

BY THE SCAFFOLD STEPS

Forrest hurried to the shed next door to his family's cottage. No bigger than a one-stall barn, the shed housed dry straw for the ravens' cages and a small worktable. It was here that Forrest chopped up the ravens' food, and it was here that Tuck spent his nights in a nest he had made for himself up in the rafters.

"You must wait in here for me, Tuck," Forrest said now, opening the shed door. "The crowds on the Hill will be great. Father says that thieves from the city will be out picking pockets and looking to steal what they can. A bird as clever as you would make a fine catch."

Tuck cocked his head and nudged Forrest's cheek with the velvety smooth top of his head.

"You'll not talk me out of it," Forrest told him firmly. "'Tis for your own good. Go on now, go on." He pointed to the rafter overhead and waited for Tuck to fly up to his favorite perch.

"I shall let you out as soon as I return," Forrest

promised. "And if I am lucky, I may leave Mother's side long enough to have an adventure!"

He shut the shed door and pulled the latch tight.

"You've finally come!" his mother cried, as he entered the cottage.

Forrest smiled as he breathed in the delicious aroma of oatcakes fresh from the fire. He looked across the room at his eight-year-old sister, Mary, who was setting the cakes to cool on a long wooden platter. Forrest's mouth watered for a taste, but before he could snatch one, his mother pulled him over to the sideboard.

"Of all days to tarry!" she exclaimed. "If we do not start soon, the crowds will be so thick we shall never be able to get close to the scaffold."

Forrest understood his mother's concern. He knew that the balladeers positioned themselves beside the scaffolds, where they sang about the criminals who were about to be executed. He also knew how much his mother loved music. She was always humming or singing a tune as she went about her chores. Except for the choir singing in the chapel on Sundays, there was little music to be heard at the Tower.

But the sounds of flutes, whistles, and drums were always to be heard on Tower Hill on a collar day. And while Forrest looked forward to the music and festivities as much as anyone, the executions themselves made him uneasy. He had no appetite for slaughter, whether of beast or man. Nonetheless, with all the hangings he'd been to, he had never actually watched a prisoner die. He always looked down at his boots at the final moment or closed his eyes.

"What's this, then?" Forrest's mother asked as she leaned over and sniffed his shirtsleeve. "Have you been sending rocks into the moat again?"

Forrest shrugged.

"Well?" his mother demanded, tapping her foot on the stone floor.

"Maybe a few," he admitted.

"Oh, you and that moat," his mother cried. "How many times must I tell you?"

Forrest groaned. It seemed unfair to have a mother with such a keen eye and so powerful a nose. As ripe as his shirt might be (for he wore it a full fourteen days between washings), his mother never failed to detect each new stain upon it.

"Have mercy on my soul," she sighed, rolling her eyes heavenward. "Your sister Mary has spilt jam on her apron, and the baby has spit up on her shift. How is it that one woman should be blessed with three of the most unkempt-looking children in all of England?"

A short while later, Mistress Harper and her "unkempt-looking children" joined the crowds that were swarming Tower Hill. Mary carried the baby as Forrest walked beside them.

He could see from the size of the crowd that his father had been right. Most of London had turned out for the execution. Thousands were arriving by horse, coach, cart, and foot. And from the crowd's jolly mood, one would hardly suspect the wretched spectacle they had come to witness.

"Mary, you hold on to Bea tightly," Forrest's mother called over the cries of a tater man, who was selling hot potatoes in their skins from a cart. "And, Forrest, make sure they stay clear of the puddles and the dung. . . ."

Forrest nodded as if he were listening. But the closer they got to the scaffold, the louder the roar of the crowd became, until finally his mother's voice resembled nothing more than the faint buzz of a pesky fly.

There was so much to hear and so much to see. It was all Forrest could do to keep an eye out for his sister, who was struggling to hold the baby atop her slender hip.

The air crackled with shouts and laughter. Dogs barked and babies cried. Forrest's head twisted from side to side as they walked past the many makeshift vendors' stands, which sold everything from ginger beer and sweet cakes to Tower rope cut by the inch and spyglasses (the "better to see the sorry sods swing").

Forrest noticed a group of boys his age who had come from the city. They talked and laughed as a juggler tossed plates into the air. Forrest longed to join them, to be part of the fun and games. He wished he had the nerve to approach them, but as they passed, they ignored him.

It is because I am so short, they think me too young to talk to, he thought miserably. *Why, they probably think I'm no older than Mary.*

To make matters worse, Bea began to move to and fro and was soon slipping so fast down her sister's hip that Mary cried out, "Forrest, help me!"

"Just pull her up!" Forrest begged.

"My arms have near given out, and I'm afraid I shall drop her," Mary complained, as the baby slid down toward her knee.

Forrest rescued the baby and looked around desperately for his mother, but she had been pushed forward by the crowd, and he couldn't get to her. He cringed as his baby sister leaned closer and drooled on his neck.

"For pity's sake, Bea," Forrest groaned, wiping his neck with his free hand. He turned to the boys, but they had moved on. Forrest looked at the crowd despondently. No other boys were there doing women's work and holding babies. His cheeks reddened with the shame of it. His hopes of meeting a friend or having any kind of adventure dimmed as he walked around with the drooling baby in his arms.

As people shoved and pushed their way closer to the scaffold, Forrest found himself beside Edward Finch and Charles Whipley, two older boys from the Tower.

"Ho there, Little Harper," Finch called. "Or should I say Mistress Harper, now that you have a baby to tend to?"

Forrest's back stiffened as the boys began to laugh.

" 'Tis fortunate your father gets only old men to guard," Whipley remarked.

"Old men, birds, and little babies," Finch laughed. "Takes a real hero to look after all that."

Forrest felt the color rise in his cheeks. "The Constable has ordered a new prisoner to come under our watch," he quickly told them.

"Another old feeble priest?" Finch taunted.

"He's neither feeble nor a priest," Forrest said hotly, "but a dangerous Jacobite Rebel taken in battle."

Forrest enjoyed the look of surprise on Finch's face.

"Look, there!" someone in the crowd shouted.

Forrest turned to see a giant of a man, dressed in a black leather apron and vest, slowly climbing the scaffold steps.

" 'Tis the Hangman!" Finch shouted.

The crowd suddenly parted as a cart pulled up beside the scaffold. The prisoner, dressed in a long greatcoat and shiny black boots, stood atop a rosewood coffin inside of the cart.

" 'Tis the Highwayman, Tom Knight!" someone cried. The prisoner was roughly pulled from the cart and led up to the scaffold.

Forrest's eyes darted to the huge, beefy-armed Hangman, who waited beside the dangling rope.

"Should be a good show, watching this one swing," Forrest heard Whipley say.

"Of course, there are those wot have no stomach for it," Finch added, giving Forrest a shove. "Young girls of delicate disposition with small children. They always shield their eyes at the opportune moment. Wot about you, Little Harper? Will you be looking down at your boots when the final moment comes?"

Forrest felt his ears begin to burn. He realized that

he was going to have to watch, for if he didn't, Whipley and Finch would surely make it known to everyone at the Tower just what a coward he was.

And as Forrest braced himself to see the man die, a balladeer stood atop a barrel and began to sing:

"Oh Hangman, stay thy hand,
And stay if for a while,
For I fancy I see my father
A-coming across yonder stile.
Oh, father, have you my gold?
And can you set me free?
Or are you come to see me hung?
All on a gallows tree?
All on a gallows tree?"

IV
HARE HEART

A hush fell over the crowd as an official read a list of the Highwayman's offenses.

"Tom Knight," the magistrate's voice boomed. "You have been brought to justice on this day for the crimes you have committed. For stealing of goods and plate . . ."

A silk rope was tied around the prisoner's neck, and a black hood was placed over his head. A collective gasp rose from the crowd. Forrest's heart pounded in his chest as he clutched little Bea tight and prayed for courage. The baby looked at him and smiled, oblivious to the horror about to unfold before her.

"Godspeed to you, Tom!" someone shouted. A cheer went up as the prisoner's courage was applauded.

"God don't want the likes of his sorry soul," someone yelled, and the crowd turned suddenly ugly. Those closest to the prisoner spat on him, while others threw rotten cabbages and onions, and the balladeers sang:

"Good night, Tom Knight, good night.
You robbed for gold and silver bright,
For to maintain your heart's delight.
Now listen to your death-bell toll,
And pray God for mercy on your soul.
Good night, Tom Knight. Good night."

A roar of laughter followed. Forrest stared straight ahead as the Highwayman was suddenly yanked into the air by the rope that squeezed and tightened around his neck. His arms and legs writhed wildly. It was neither a quick nor painless death.

Forrest's mouth went dry when a wild-eyed woman suddenly climbed onto the scaffold. A ripple of whispers swept through the crowd as she reached up and began to frantically pull on the prisoner's legs.

" 'Tis the Highwayman's lady love," Forrest heard someone behind him say. "She hopes to end his agony the sooner."

The woman cried out in desperation as his body continued to jerk in pain. Forrest felt his stomach lurch at the sight of it, and before he could stop himself, he leaned forward and heaved up his breakfast.

"Have a look at little Mistress Harper now!" Whipley cried. "He sickens like a girl!"

"He's just a frightened little hare," exclaimed Finch, clasping his hands to his chest and batting his eyes.

As Forrest looked up, the boys' laughter rose up around him.

"Hare Heart!" Whipley shouted. "There's a new name for Mistress Harper. From now on he shall be known as the little rabbit, little Hare Heart!"

Hare Heart, Hare Heart, Hare Heart. The hated words repeated over and over in Forrest's head.

He trudged back down the hill toward home in silence as his mother, with Bea now safely in her arms, chattered with Mary about the different frocks and bonnets they'd seen, the puddings they'd eaten, and the music they'd heard. But Forrest could hear nothing but the shameful nickname repeating over and over in his mind.

If only he could have answered the bullies. But he had been too ashamed to speak.

As they headed down the muddy hill, Forrest could see the fortress before them, its towers rising up in hard-edged stone within the curtain walls. He quickly picked out the weather vanes atop the turrets on the White Tower. It was the oldest and most formidable building in the fortress, standing at nearly ninety feet tall with walls that were fifteen feet thick. His father had told him all about William the

Conqueror and how he had built the first Norman Keep after conquering the Saxon armies. Ever since, the Tower had been a symbol of the courage and strength of the great kings and queens of England.

As they walked, Forrest wondered how William the Conqueror would have answered the bullies. He wondered if William's stomach had ever churned as he watched a hanging. But he didn't have to wonder if the Warrior King had ever shown weakness, for he knew the answer was surely never.

V
STRENGTH AND WEAKNESS

That night Forrest was unable to sleep. As he lay awake in his sleeping loft, he tried counting the chirps of a cricket that sang from the rafter overhead. It didn't help. Nor did counting the drips of rain that leaked through the cottage roof.

The loud *clang, clang, clang* from the Bell Tower echoed through the still night. The curfew bell was a signal to workmen and visitors that the Tower was closing. All gates would soon be locked and the drawbridges raised. No one would be allowed into the fortress until morning. Both prisoners and their guards were locked in tight.

Forrest closed his eyes and tried to imagine what it must be like to be one of those visitors to the Tower. How did it feel to know that, if you wanted to, you could cross that drawbridge and never come back? What must it be like to be free of the fortress's stony grip forever? As the son of a Yeoman Warder, he could never know such freedom. His parents had grown so accustomed to life in the Tower that they rarely went outside to the city. And Forrest was not allowed to cross the drawbridge without them.

He opened his eyes and listened now. The bell had stopped ringing. A deadly quiet followed, and his mind returned to the scene on the hill. A wave of if onlys tormented him.

If only I weren't so much smaller than all the other boys. If only I hadn't been holding Bea. If only I had had the courage to watch the Highwayman swing! If only, if only, if only . . .

When he heard his father's paper rustling from below, Forrest tiptoed to the loft's ladder. In the glow of the firelight, he could just make out the lump in his parents' bed, where his mother lay snoring under her coverlet. Bea and Mary slept soundly in a little wooden bed beside her.

On the other side of the room, a rush lamp burned. Forrest's father sat in his favorite chair, reading his penny paper before the fire with Nubbins, the family cat, on his lap. In the lamplight, the Ravenmaster's silver beard and spectacles made him look older than his forty-five years.

Wearing only his nightshirt, Forrest climbed down the worn rungs of the hickory ladder. His father's bushy eyebrows shot up on seeing him. Nubbins yawned as his eye opened a crack.

"'Tis late for you to be up," the Ravenmaster said softly, peering over his spectacles.

"I couldn't sleep," Forrest told him, as he stepped closer to the fire. The hearth's warm bricks felt good under his cold feet.

"You take after me there," his father said. "Sleep has never come easy to me, and yet no sooner does your mother lay down her head on a feather bed, she's gone to the world. Why, just listen to the woman!"

They both smiled at the steady snoring that filled the room.

"And what do you think of our birds?" his father asked. "Have you noticed all the new nest-making going on of late? I'll wager we'll have some fine fledglings this year."

"Aye," Forrest agreed. He usually loved the conversations about the ravens that only the two of them could have. But tonight he had something else on his mind.

"I wish I took after you in other ways," he blurted out. "I wish I was big like you, instead of so small like Mother."

"And why is that?" his father sighed.

"For then the other boys would have no cause to call me names and bully me," Forrest hurried to explain. "You don't know what it's like to be me."

"No, I cannot know what it is like to be you," his father agreed. "But I do know that a man's greatness cannot be measured by his size. 'Tis a man's character that is the source of his strength. And weakness there cannot be hidden."

Forrest bristled. "Who said I was weak?"

"I was speaking of those boys who bullied you," his father said. " 'Tis their own weakness that drives them to torment others. I dare say, by wishing to change yourself to please them, why, you've only given them power over you."

"But how can I get them to stop?"

"It's quite simple, really," his father said. "Ignore them."

" 'Twould be simpler if I were bigger and older," Forrest sighed. "For then I could leave the Tower and go to live in the city."

His father smiled. "Any coward can run away. It takes more courage to listen to your own voice and claim what is rightfully yours. Your home is here at the Tower. You will be Ravenmaster one day. But the place you need to go now is to your bed, for our new prisoner is arriving tomorrow. So off with you, boy. Try to get some sleep."

Later that night, as Forrest lay back under his quilt, listening to the patter of the rain on the roof, he thought about the bullies and the power they had over him. His father made it sound so easy to be strong, but Forrest knew it wasn't.

Perhaps the new prisoner would be the answer to his problems. If this Rebel Scot were big enough and fierce enough, perhaps the bullies would respect him.

Forrest fell into a fitful sleep. His dreams were full of bullies and babies and William the Conqueror.

Meanwhile, twelve miles to the north, two captured Rebel Scots lay wide awake on a bed of donkey straw. As their guards nodded off on the other side of a barred door, the two busily plotted their escape.

"Tomorrow we reach the Tower," one whispered. "And I'll wager the King's executioner is already sharpening his blade. If there is a way out of that godforsaken prison, we must find it, for if we're to die on English soil, I say we do not go without a fight. Are we agreed?"

There was no hesitation. The other whispered firmly.

"Agreed."

VI
RAT

As the early morning light streamed in through the wide cracks in the shed's oak siding, Forrest was busy inside with his chores. He threw down a layer of fresh straw over the dirt floor. But the good, clean scent of new straw could not hide the sickening sweet smell of dead rodents that filled the air. Breakfast for the birds.

Of all his chores, preparing the ravens' meals was the task Forrest had the least liking for. As he picked up a knife on the table, he recalled his father's words.

"If you're to understand ravens, you must learn to understand the ways of nature," his father had said, as he showed Forrest how to chop up a squirrel.

"Each of us feeds on something. This squirrel has eaten its fill and lived its life; now it is food for another. If you're to be Ravenmaster one day, you will need steady hands, for you must cut off many heads to feed your charges. The ravens must eat fresh kill and blood-soaked biscuits to keep strong."

And so Forrest had learned never to look into the

squirrel's eyes or into any of the eyes of the fresh kill that made up the ravens' daily meals. Although his hands no longer shook, his stomach still lurched as he maneuvered the knife.

Tuck's loud "I'm hungry" squawk rang out from outside the shed.

"Yes, yes, your breakfast is coming," Forrest grumbled as he gingerly cut up a fresh mouse.

Suddenly, the shed door creaked open, and the strong scent of cloves filled the air.

Forrest smiled. He knew of only one person who smelled so strongly of that spice, and it was his friend Rat. Forrest looked up now to see the small, barefoot boy enter the shed. Rat's ragged jacket was full of stains. His tangled hair poked out from under a tattered blue cap, and his face was smudged with dirt. He held a small club in one hand and a dirty old sack in the other.

"Oh, Rat, am I ever glad to see you!" Forrest exclaimed.

Rat's nickname and his spicy scent came with his occupation, for he was apprenticed to Barnabas Meeks, the Tower's Official Rat Catcher. He had only been at the Tower for several months, having spent his earlier days catching rats in the houses along the river.

"Every rat catcher knows that rats love the smell of

cloves," Rat had once explained to Forrest. "And so every week Master Meeks soaks a part of me jacket in clove oil. With me being so small, I can fit into cupboards and tight spaces, where rats likes to nest. The smell of me jacket draws 'um out, and I kills 'um with me club or we sic our ferret Bill on 'um. Either way they end up in me bag."

Because he was so dirty and because he was an orphan who spent his days catching rats, none of the other children at the Tower ever spoke to Rat, except to shout insults at him. And mothers warned their children to stay clear of him.

Forrest's own mother had called him a "dirty little urchin" and complained about his coming around so much. But since the ravens needed fresh kill daily, the Ravenmaster had worked out an arrangement with Barnabas Meeks. Each day, his apprentice was to drop off a bag of fresh-killed rodents at the Harpers' shed.

At first, Forrest kept his distance from the little rat catcher, and the two boys never spoke. It was Tuck who finally brought them together. For the raven took an instant liking to Rat, greeting him with his friendliest calls and often dropping "presents" down on his head, a copper nail or a bit of tin. Tuck loved anything shiny, and he hoarded his finds in his nest on a rafter in the shed. Forrest knew that his pet didn't part with these treasures easily and would never make a present of them to someone he didn't trust. Yet here he was giving them to the little rat catcher!

Tuck seemed to take no notice of how dirty Rat looked or how ragged his clothes were. It was as if the raven could see past all that, into the very heart of the boy. He seemed to like what he saw. And so Forrest began to take a closer look as well. He saw how patient and gentle Rat was with Tuck. When the raven suddenly flew onto the small boy's shoulder one day, Rat didn't flinch or try to shake him off but only smiled and said, "There's a good bird."

Forrest noticed something else about Rat. One afternoon, as he was walking along Water Lane, Forrest spotted the little rat catcher kneeling beside a wall. As Forrest stepped closer, he could see that the boy was drawing a perfect-looking catapult on the wall's face with a piece of charcoal.

The next day Forrest decided to draw a catapult of his own on the shed wall. He was having trouble with his drawing, when Rat stopped in to drop off his catch.

"I can't get it right," Forrest complained aloud.

Without saying a word, the little rat catcher pulled a piece of charcoal from his pocket and corrected the picture. Soon the two worked side by side, creating a battle scene filled with catapults, knights, horses, and even a dragon. Conversations about ravens and rats soon followed, and a friendship began.

The more the boys talked, the more they discovered how alike they were. They were both small and quick. They both loved to draw battles. And they both loved birds, Tuck being their favorite. But it was the spyglass that truly sealed their friendship. For everyone else who had ever looked through the glass always mentioned how cloudy and useless it was. That is, everyone but Rat. One day, as Forrest held it to his eye and imagined aloud the wide ocean he saw through it, Rat asked to have a look. Forrest hesitated at first but handed it over and silently watched as Rat held it up to his eye. Neither boy spoke.

"Lor', 'tis jest as big an ocean as you said," Rat finally whispered. Forrest knew then that they were meant to be friends, for they could both see what others could not.

As fond as he was of imaginary places, Forrest was also eager to hear about real life, especially life outside the Tower. He pestered Rat to tell him all he could about what happened when he left the fortress each day. There was little to tell, for Rat didn't live in the city, but rather in the area along the river just beside the fortress walls. When he wasn't catching rats at the Tower, the orphan spent his nights sleeping alone on a pallet in the dank, dark cellar of Barnabas Meeks's house. He was given no candles and was never invited upstairs.

Forrest knew that he could never invite Rat inside his house, either. The son of a Yeoman Warder could never be seen keeping company with an orphaned rat catcher. But since Rat stopped by the shed each day on business, there was plenty of opportunity for their friendship to grow. Together they drew battles in secret on the shed wall or looked through the old spyglass and imagined themselves on amazing adventures.

Forrest waited for Rat to shut the shed door. He was anxious to tell him all about the bullies and what had happened on the Hill.

"I don't blame you for not looking," Rat sympathized, once he'd heard the whole story. "I always get a sick feeling in me stomach to see 'um swing. And I always think, wot if it was me own neck in that noose?"

Forrest let out a sigh of relief on hearing this. "I've never been easy with killing," he admitted. "I pray that will change, but it never does. What kind of boy hasn't the courage to kill? Even chopping up this rat still makes me uneasy." He frowned as he stared down at the dead animal on his board.

"Oh, I kills rats all day. I shouldn't fret about chopping one up," Rat told him. "I could help you with that rat if you like. Though I might need to stand on your bucket to reach the table."

As short as Forrest was, Rat was shorter still. Forrest quickly grabbed the bucket and turned it over.

"'Tis my curst luck to be so small," Rat muttered, climbing up to the table. "And Master Meeks keeps threatening to sell me to the Tower's chimney sweep if I don't catch him more rats."

Forrest shuddered, for his father had told him stories of the London sweeps and how they preyed on smaller children, kidnapping them for slaves and forcing them to climb up the city's many dangerous chimneys that needed cleaning. "Most climbing boys don't live to see their beards come in," his father had said.

Forrest understood now just how brave Rat must be to live alone in the world, with no father to protect him from the cruel ways of Barnabas Meeks and his threats.

"We're getting a new prisoner," Forrest suddenly declared. "A Scottish Rebel. My father says that he was probably taken in battle. I'll dare those boys to make fun of our prisoner now."

"I've heard Master Meeks say that those from up north are a wild breed of men," Rat said, as he picked up a knife and began chopping.

"Aye, I've heard the same," Forrest agreed. "Warder

Thomas says they are all the same. Hard-boiled and low-minded. And when they do think at all, 'tis only to plot treason."

Rat looked up from the worktable. "Can they speak English?"

"No," Forrest said, shaking his head. "They speak in a strange twisted tongue. And I've heard talk of how the Highlanders eat their animals whole. Bone, fur, and all. Why, Master Nutly, the cobbler, said that some even foam at the mouth!"

Rat cringed. "I'd rather catch rats."

"Have you ever got bit by one?" Forrest asked.

Rat flinched at the question and pointed down to his blackened left toe. "This scar 'ere," he said, bending down to wipe the dirt from it, "come from a river rat. They're the worst, they are. Why, that pain was so fierce it traveled from me toe clear up to me ear! Had to take to bed for three days with the sickness from it."

"Have you never thought of running away?" whispered Forrest.

Rat sighed. "Thought of it, dreamed of it. But Master Meeks, he owns me for seven years indenture. As hard as me life is with him, 'tis better than 'avin' to climb up them horrid chimneys. I'm lucky to be a rat catcher, I am."

"And when your indenture is done," Forrest persisted, "what will you do then?"

Rat pushed his old blue cap back on his head. "I don't rightly know what I'll do. Master Meeks bought me from the foundling home when I was six years of age. I'm almost ten now, so I've three years left to work for him. I ain't never been on me own. But in truth, if I could go anywhere I chose, I'd find me a place wot had few rats and no chimneys. Do you suppose there is such a place?"

"A place far from the Tower?" Forrest asked softly, as he pulled his spyglass from its case.

"Aye," Rat answered. "A place wot is always warm and 'as plenty of food to eat. A place where there's no master to beat your back when your bag ain't full. Can you see such a place through your glass?"

Forrest put his eye to the cloudy lens and nodded. "Aye, I think I see it!" he whispered. "'Tis just there, have a look."

VII

TORN FROM THE BONE

As the two friends were busy looking through the old spyglass, Tuck was busy watching the person walking toward them, just beyond the wall. Tuck, being a raven, had a keen intuition about character. He had known to befriend Rat long before Forrest ever did. And it wasn't just a good character that he could pick out. He could spot a bad character as well. As Forrest and Rat sat imagining themselves in some far-off land, Tuck's throat hackles went up and he opened his bill, for he had just spotted a bad character, a very, very, *very* bad character.

"*Kek-kek-kek!*" the raven cried in alarm.

The boys spun around as the crunch of gravel under boots sounded behind them. Forrest felt his mouth go dry at the sight of the stooped figure coming toward them. It was Simon Frick, the Tower's chimney sweep.

He was dressed in various shades of black, from his stained stove-pipe hat down to his old, cracked, hobnailed boots. Tall, gangly, and wafer thin, he carried an assortment of brooms and pokers over his shoulder. Forrest couldn't help but notice how the gray skin on the sweep's long face looked as if it had been pulled too tightly across his cheeks, giving him a menacing, corpselike look. His sharp, hooked nose was streaked with grime.

But as frightful as the sweep appeared, the three shadowy figures following close behind were even more ghastly. Only from the size of their stunted little bodies could one guess that they must be children. Whether boys or girls Forrest couldn't tell. The few rags that clothed their brittle little bones were layered with filth. Like ash-covered ghouls they trailed the sweep, moving in a trancelike state, looking more dead than alive. Forrest winced at the sight of their great hollowed eyes, reddened and runny from the smoky chimneys they climbed.

Swift as a spider, Frick drew closer. Forrest and Rat instantly recoiled, almost falling backward off the wall.

"A happy coincidence meeting you lads today," the sweep wheezed in a sickly sweet voice. Years of sucking in soot had left him gasping for breath. "I was 'oping' to make your acquaintance."

"Us?" croaked Forrest. "You were hoping to meet us?"

The sweep nodded and turned to Rat. "You especially," he hissed. "I've been speaking to your Master Meeks about you. For I think you might be just the boy I'm looking for." With that, he leaned in closer to the wall, then tapped Rat's head with the tip of his spindly finger.

"And yes! By jolly, just the boy. For you are surely small enough. Tell me, boy, 'ave you ever climbed up a chimney?"

"Ne . . . never!" Rat answered, shaken.

"Well, that may change," Simon Frick said with a ghastly grin. "Yes, that may very well change."

Rat's face went white as he clutched Forrest's arm.

"Go back up your chimney," Forrest muttered under his breath.

"Were you speaking to me, boy?" the sweep demanded with a frosty stare.

"No, sir. I was just talking to my raven."

Simon Frick's soulless gray eyes rolled toward the raven and back to Forrest, giving him a look so sharp and piercing, Forrest let out a small cry.

But what lifted the hairs on the back of his neck was the sight of the sweep pulling a knife from a sheath at his waist.

"Lie to me, and I will know it," Simon Frick hissed. He clicked his long blackened nails on the knife's blade. "Interfere with what is mine or about to be mine . . ." He shot a look at Rat and then turned back to Forrest. "And you will regret the day you did. Me climbing boys are me property, you see," the sweep said in a wheezy whisper. He took a long broom from his shoulder and used it to poke one of his charges. A weak groan sounded from the little heap of rags.

Simon Frick sneered and turned back to Forrest. "Do you take me meaning, boy?"

Rat was still clutching Forrest as the sweep leaned back over and put the knife's sharp blade to Forrest's cheek.

"Yes, sir," Forrest whispered.

The sweep's eyes flashed back to Tuck. And his thin gray lips curled into a malicious little smile.

"Ah, yes, birds! Rather fond of them meself," he whispered. "Ever tasted raven, lad?"

Forrest felt a sickly twist in his stomach.

"Turned slow on a spit." The sweep licked his lips with the tip of his green-tinged tongue. "The meat torn from the bone. I hear it makes a tasty meal," he cackled, as he swung his broom over his shoulder and walked away. The three shadowy figures trailed at his heels.

"Most tasty, most tasty."

VIII
THE PRISONER

All day long, as Forrest did his chores, he couldn't get the frightening image of the old sweep and the ghostly climbing boys out of his mind. Neither could he stop thinking of Rat and of how much more horrible his life could turn if his master decided to sell him. Now Forrest understood what Rat had meant when he said he was lucky to be a rat catcher.

In the meantime, Forrest had no luck in escaping his chores. He groaned as he heaved a piece of wood onto a mountain of kindling behind his family's cottage. "I shall be an old man before I ever get all this wood stacked."

Tuck answered with a sympathetic warble from his perch atop the woodpile. Forrest reached into his pocket and pulled out a small tin circle, the size of a coin. Whenever the tinsmith visited the Tower, Forrest would beg for any scraps that the smith had no use for.

"Come on, Tuck," he called now, throwing the shiny disk in the air. "Get it, boy."

The raven flew to the disk and caught it in his beak. Teaching Tuck tricks was much more interesting than doing chores, so Forrest often stopped his work to practice a new one. He pulled a dirty old rag from his pocket and threw it up into the air. The raven swooped down and grabbed the rag in his beak.

"Good boy." Forrest smiled. "Now, give it back."

Tuck flew up onto the roof instead, the rag still dangling from his beak.

"No, Tuck!" Forrest scolded. "You are supposed to return it to me." But he could not get the raven's attention.

In total frustration, Forrest hoisted up his legs and stood on his head.

"Look here, Tuck!" he called to the bird. "Look at me, I'm upside down."

"And you'd best get yourself right side up if you know what's good for you," his mother ordered from above.

Forrest tumbled to the ground. "I was just doing some . . ."

"Never mind what you were doing," his mother fumed. "'Tis what you were *not* doing that concerns me. Why, you've hardly stacked any kindling, and the afternoon is near over! You can't spend all your time daydreaming and playing with that raven, for there's work to be . . ."

Her lecture was cut short by a dirty old rag that suddenly came floating down from above and landed on her head.

"What in Heaven's name?" she cried.

"Sorry, Mother," Forrest whispered, as he reached up for the rag. " 'Tis a new trick that Tuck is learning."

"Enough of your tricks," his mother scolded, shaking her head. "Your father wants you to go down to Traitor's Gate."

Forrest's dark eyes brightened, for he knew that the ancient gateway off Water Lane was the entrance for those prisoners arriving by boat.

"Aye, Mother, I'll leave now."

"You are to tell Warder Simms that your father is on his way. And here," she said, reaching into her apron. "Your sister made these ginger biscuits this morning, though you don't deserve a treat, I daresay." She handed him two cookies.

"Thank you, Mother." Forrest grinned as he put one cookie into his pocket and took a bite out of the other. Then he whistled two long whistles.

"Come on, Tuck," he called. Within seconds, the raven glided down and landed on Forrest's shoulder.

Together the two made their way past the warders' smoking cottages nestled in the outer curtain walls. They dodged chickens and pigs and warders' wives, who gathered to gossip behind the bed linens they were airing.

They passed warders who stood guard or tended to official Tower business in their familiar crimson uniforms. And from up on the battlements, they could see prisoners dressed in velvet and satin walking on the ramparts. These were the prisoners who were not held "close." They were given "the liberty of the Tower" and were allowed out of their cells to take the morning air.

The Tower grounds were also filling with the usual collection of tradesmen who came from the city to sell their wares. They passed a pockmarked man carrying a bundle of kindling on his back and a young girl pulling a cow by a rope.

When they finally reached the cobbled street of Water Lane, Forrest could hear the rhythmic clatter of boots hitting cobblestones. He looked over at the Byward Tower to see a battalion of the King's soldiers marching toward them. He quickly found Warder Simms and delivered his father's message.

Then he walked up to a small group of workmen, who had gathered to catch a glimpse of the boat that would dock under the large stone arch of Traitor's Gate.

"Business? Why, business is booming!" a familiar

voice bellowed. "For there's no better place on earth to find vermin. 'Tis a rat catcher's dream, this old Tower is."

Forrest turned to see Master Meeks talking with a red-faced mason. Rat was standing beside him. When the old rat catcher caught sight of Forrest, he grinned and waved him over with a large hand, crisscrossed with scratches and scars. Forrest nodded uneasily, as Tuck warbled nervously from his shoulder, for Barnabas Meeks was a frightening figure. He was a big-muscled man with little black, ratlike eyes and a yellow-toothed grin over his grizzled beard. It was said that he killed rats with his bare hands.

"Come and tell me, lad," Master Meeks barked at Forrest, "how are them ravens of yours finding our vermin? Are they tasty enough for 'um?"

"Aye, sir, I suppose they are," Forrest replied.

"Satisfied customers, that's wot we likes to hear." Meeks chortled as he turned back to the workman.

Meanwhile Forrest inched his way to Rat's side.

"Have you seen any more of the sweep today?" Forrest whispered.

Rat shook his head no. But his forehead was wrinkled with worry.

"Make way, make way," a warder shouted.

Forrest and Rat stepped back along with the crowd, as the King's soldiers approached.

The two boys grew quiet as the boat docked, and they spotted the first prisoner being led ashore in chains. Forrest held his breath. It was too good to be true! The Rebel Scot was huge. Big and burly with massive shoulders and hands great enough to tear a man in two. And even though he wore a plaid skirt instead of trousers, he carried himself with a fierce pride, the pride of a warrior.

"His heart must be pounding in his chest," Rat whispered.

"Aye," Forrest agreed. "For he knows full well, without a pardon from the King, there are only two means of escape for them now: the yank of the rope or the slice of the axe."

Forrest could hardly contain his excitement when the second prisoner appeared looking much like the first, except that he had a jagged cut across his forehead. The wound was crusted over with dried blood and dirt, and an angry red welt had formed all along its edges. Rat gasped at the sight of it.

"A pretty mark there on your head, Scotsman," one of the workmen yelled out. "Was it an English sword wot gave it to you?"

"If it was, it should have finished the job properly and taken his whole sorry head off!" another workman shouted.

This was met with a roar of laughter. The prisoner muttered something in Gaelic, then spit in the direction of the crowd.

"Mercy, they are as fierce as I had hoped for! Big and wild looking, too," Forrest whispered to Rat.

A third prisoner who followed the men was a young girl. She looked to be about Forrest's age, eleven or twelve years old, he guessed. She was wearing a long, green woolen cape and was in chains as well. Her clear blue eyes were fixed directly ahead of her. And like the men before her, this girl had the unmistakable bearing of nobility.

As she drew closer, the wind blew back her cape and Forrest could see a small bunch of heather tucked into the sash of her dress. When she suddenly tripped and almost fell to the ground, she neither cried nor called out. But Forrest could see that her lower lip had begun to tremble. It was only a quiver, but the sight of it pierced his heart. He wished he could offer her a hand, though he knew he mustn't.

As she tried to stand, their eyes met for an instant. Her gaze was so fierce, so determined, he had to look away. When he looked back, she and the soldiers beside her had moved on.

"Well, lad, you've had your look," the Ravenmaster said, coming up behind Forrest. "I'll be needing you to fetch a mug up to the Bloody Tower. Once you are finished feeding the birds, tell your mother to brew a pot of tea for our prisoner. I daresay the little wench will be chilled after her long journey."

"Wench?" Forrest croaked. "Did you say 'wench,' Father?"

"Aye, I've just had word. Seems our Scot's skirts are longer than most," his father replied. "The girl's father is Owen Stewart, a known Scottish Rebel. He and her uncle have both been charged with treason. The girl's been charged as well. I wonder what your mother will have to say when she hears that our prisoner is a Scottish Rebel's daughter."

But as he watched his father walk away, all Forrest could think about was what Finch and the others would say once they heard that their new prisoner was a girl.

IX
Through the Spyglass

The raven's cages stood beside a low wall in the inner ward just off the Tower green.

"Cursed," Forrest groaned, as he kicked the wall. "Surely I must be cursed."

The ravens all hurried over to the wall at the sound of his voice.

"Stunning bad luck," Rat agreed, as he sat down beside him. With his catching done for the day, Rat was free to make his way home by himself. Master Meeks had decided to celebrate his "booming business" by stopping at the alehouse just outside the Tower walls. But Rat often stayed at the Tower as long as he could, rather than return to his dungeonlike cellar.

"*Kee . . . kee . . . kee,*" one of the ravens called to them now, from the ground where Forrest had thrown them some horse meat.

Forrest shot the bird a sour look. " 'Tis all right for you, Thor," he grumbled. "For you're head bird. No one thinks you a coward nor is calling you Hare Heart.

And I shudder to think what new names they'll come up with when they find out about our new prisoner."

" 'Twould 'ave been better if she were foaming at the mouth," Rat said, shaking his head.

"It won't matter to Finch and the others whether she's foaming or not," Forrest moaned. "She's a girl! 'Twill be one more thing they can use to mock me. When I'm finished here, I'm to stop home and fetch her a mug of tea. Can you imagine what the others will say when they find out that I'm fetching tea for a girl?"

"They ain't worth your worry," Rat said, as he tried to console him. "If I was you . . ."

"But you are not me!" Forrest snapped. "You are not a warder's son. Nothing is expected of you. You are just . . ."

He stopped suddenly seeing the pinched, hurt look on Rat's face.

"Just a rat catcher," Rat finished his sentence.

"I'm sorry," Forrest said, staring at his boots.

"You're right, of course," Rat said, shrugging off the apology. "I ain't one of you Tower boys." Neither spoke then until Forrest remembered the ginger biscuit in his pocket. He quickly took it out and offered it to Rat, hoping to make up for the slight.

"My sister Mary made it," he explained. " 'Tis not as good as Mother makes. But 'tisn't too bad, either."

Rat's face brightened on seeing the biscuit. "Don't rightly care who made it," he said, taking a bite out of it. "Ain't never 'ad a full plate under Master Meeks's roof, much less a ginger biscuit. I'll save the rest to eat for me supper," he said, as he shoved the biscuit into his pocket.

As a flock of geese flew overhead, the boys watched them circle over the White Tower, then the Broad Arrow Tower, swinging over Water Lane, and finally disappearing behind Traitor's Gate and beyond the many turrets, towers, and stone walls that encircled them.

"So free," Forrest heard Rat whisper under his breath.

The fog had begun to drift in off the river. Forrest turned up his collar and wrinkled his nose as the stink from the moat was strong in the damp, chilly air.

Forrest watched as the other ravens hopped over to the wall to see what all the commotion was about.

"With such great wings," Rat said, "'tis a shame the ravens can't use them to fly."

"They could never make it over the Tower's walls," Forrest told him. "For their wings are clipped when they are young."

"But Tuck could," Rat pointed out. "Do you never wonder why it is that he don't fly away?"

Forrest looked at Tuck, who was busy scratching his head with his foot. "I've raised him from a fledgling, and he's happy here with me, I suppose. But I'll tell you this," he said, lowering his voice to a whisper. "If I were a wild raven and could fly anywhere I chose, why, I'd fly as far over these walls as I could get."

"Where would you fly to then?" whispered Rat.

"Into the city and beyond," Forrest said dreamily. "Why, there is a whole world outside London. A world where a boy could prove his courage. Of course, I'll never get to see it, stuck here in this Tower as I am."

"I shouldn't complain if I was you," Rat told him. "Living as you do in a nice warm cottage, with parents to look after you and a raven of your own. Why, most boys would give their boots to be in your place. If they had boots that is."

Forrest looked down at Rat's dirty bare feet. Then he looked up above the White Tower's turrets to the billowy clouds overhead. And his eyes suddenly shone as his lips formed a smile.

"Imagine us out in the world, together. You, me, and Tuck," he whispered excitedly. "We could be on a clipper ship, setting out for the New World." He took his spyglass out of its case and held it up to his eye.

Rat grinned. "Aye, and I'll 'ave me a sword with a gold hilt and a parrot to ride on me shoulder."

"And you shall have silver buckles on your boots," Forrest added.

"I'll 'ave boots?" Rat grinned, as he wiggled his outstretched toes.

"Of course you shall have boots," Forrest assured him. "All sea captains have boots. And you'll have a nasty scar on your face as well. Right about there," he said, reaching out to touch Rat's cheek with his finger.

Rat frowned. "A scar? I don't much like the sound of that. How'd I come by this scar?" he asked, holding a dirty hand to his face.

"From a dagger fight with a pirate, of course!" Forrest told him.

"And did I 'ave to throw 'im overboard?" Rat asked, his green eyes twinkling with delight.

Forrest nodded. "Yes, and you took that nasty scar on your cheek as a reminder. Here, have a look through my glass. You can see the deserted pirate ship still, tossing out at sea."

"Someday, we'll travel beyond these old walls and towers," Forrest said. "You'll see."

The sudden sharp sound of a bugle echoed across the Green and pulled the boys out of their daydream. It was a call Forrest had heard every day of his life, signaling the changing of the guards. He knew that the King's men would be marching, stiff as toy soldiers, into their little black guardhouses.

The daily routines of the Tower never changed. They were unwavering in their order, set in mortar and stone, and tended to by the dutiful Yeoman Warders. And though it was an order that Forrest had always loved, more and more often, he longed to be free of it.

"There is so much to see in the world," he whispered to Rat, as he peered through the glass. "Why, there's a mountain with a castle built on its peak!"

"Let me look," Rat pleaded. "Let me look."

Forrest handed him the spyglass, and the two were off on another adventure.

X
Ghosts in the Bloody Tower

"What are you doing wasting time with that old glass when there's still work to be done?" Forrest's father demanded. "Get yourself home and fetch that tea up to the new prisoner this minute."

Forrest sprang from the wall. "Aye, Father," he called. "I'm going now."

"If only you'd spend half as much time working as you spend daydreaming . . . ," his father muttered, and he walked away abruptly.

Forrest frowned. "I've got to hurry home," he said to Rat. "But will you come to the Bloody Tower with me? I've never had to tend to a girl prisoner before, and surely I could use your help."

Rat shrugged. "I suppose I could. But I heard that the Bloody Tower is haunted."

"Aye," said Forrest. "It is. Old Master Marsh says he's seen enough spirits there to turn his blood to white-wine vinegar."

"I wouldn't want no spirits to turn my blood to vinegar," Rat said, clutching his club.

"They won't if you stick with me," Forrest said. "Do come with me. I shouldn't be long. I'll meet you at the Tower door."

Ten minutes later, as he stopped to steal a sip of tea from the prisoner's mug, Forrest saw Rat waiting for him under the wide stone arch before the Bloody Tower. The hot tea tasted good in the damp, chilly air. Forrest thought about taking another sip. He knew that some prisoners were so rich that they ate and drank better than their guards. They paid for good meat and fine wines to be brought in for them.

He wondered how wealthy the Scottish girl was. Her fine velvet-trimmed cape and good leather boots told him that she was not poor. And how powerful was her family? He would find out soon enough. In the meantime, Forrest hurried to the Tower doors where Rat was waiting.

"Hallo, young Harper," called Warder Marsh, who stood guard in the gate passage. "What's your business here today?"

"Come with a mug and a crust for the new prisoner," Forrest told him, as he held up the mug and a small half-loaf of bread.

"Oh, aye, and I see the little rat catcher has come as well. He'll fill his bag from this Tower, I'll warrant. Lord Hampton has been grumbling of vermin eating his vittles, and they're so plentiful in the Duke of Sheffield's cell, they've taken to chewing the leather covers clear off his books."

"And when you're through here," Warder Thomas added, "tell your master to send you back to the Byward Tower for there's a rat there bigger than any cat I know. Remind your Master, now."

"Aye, I will," Rat promised.

"Here is the key to your prisoner's cell," Warder Marsh said to Forrest. He took a key off an iron ring. "I'd go up and unlock it myself, but you should be able to handle a little wench on your own." He winked at Warder Thomas, who was standing beside him.

Forrest grew angry at the joke, but silently took the key. He and Rat hurried through the Tower's entrance, and their eyes narrowed to adjust to the darkness. With Tuck contentedly perched on his shoulder, Forrest led the way up the winding staircase. Rat followed close behind. The only light to guide them came from the dusty sunbeams filtering through the arrow slits in the Tower's thick walls.

Forrest turned around to see Rat pressing his trembling hand against the cold Tower wall to steady himself.

The clammy touch of the stones' ancient gloom seemed to go right through the little fellow, causing him to shudder. They climbed higher and higher.

"It is said that the mortar of this place is mixed with blood," Forrest called over his shoulder.

Rat yanked his hand away from the wall. "I 'ope none of our blood is left 'ere," he said nervously.

Forrest sank down onto a step to rest as Tuck clung to his shoulder.

" 'Av we far to go?" Rat asked, as he sat down beside him.

"We're almost halfway up," Forrest said.

"How can you tell?"

"I know we're halfway because of that step there," Forrest explained. He pointed down to a step that was twice as deep as the others. Tuck stretched out his neck to look.

"So why is this step so much bigger?" Rat asked.

"The Normans built it that way," Forrest explained. " 'Tis extra deep to thwart those trying to enter and those trying to escape. For whether it be an enemy rushing up or a prisoner rushing down, why, they'd be thrown off balance when they reached this one step with its extra drop. And with no handholds to grab on to, they'd most likely take a terrible tumble and die."

"And how many ghosts do you suppose have flown up these steps?" Rat whispered.

"Legions, according to Master Marsh," Forrest said. "He saw two on this very stairwell one snowy Sunday at Even Fall. Said they gave him such a fright, his beard turned from red to white that very moment. Ghost boys they were."

"Ghost boys!" gasped Rat. "You mean they were young ghosts? Young like you and me?"

"Aye," Forrest replied. "But not lowborn, for these had been boys of royal blood, princes they were. And it was their own uncle, the wicked King Richard, who had them murdered while they slept above."

"Murdered," croaked Rat, his forehead wrinkled with worry. "Here?"

"Aye. 'Tis why they began to call this tower the Bloody Tower. It all happened some three hundred years past. I've thought of them often as I've had to climb these steps. And I've wondered if I should ever get a chance to see them."

Another noise, louder than the first, sounded from above. Tuck shifted nervously on Forrest's shoulder as a shrill cry echoed down to them,

"Deliver me from this darkness! A living death is what this is!"

"'Av mercy on my soul! Who's that then?" cried Rat. He threw his hands up over his eyes. "Is it the ghost princes come to haunt us?"

"Nay," Forrest assured him. "'Tis the Countess Asbury from her cell above. She screams and cries nearly every morn. She's been a prisoner now for almost four years. She's gone mad in the head, she has."

"Help me! God help me!" the woman cried.

"Lor', if I 'ad to spend me days and nights alone in this Bloody Tower, with ghost boys floating about, why, I'd be screaming me lungs out, too! Your new prisoner must be scared out of her wits."

"But she's not like you and me," Forrest reminded him, as he leaned forward and cocked his head to listen. "For she is not English. She's a Scot."

"I hope she ain't crying or carrying on like the countess, for I should hate to hear that," Rat said anxiously.

"Well, if she is . . ."

But his words trailed off as he heard wailing in the distance. Tuck's throat hackles suddenly puffed out, and his jet-black eyes blinked rapidly at the sound of a strange new voice.

"What is it, hey?" Forrest whispered to the bird. "Do you hear something? Is it a ghost?"

As the voice echoed and drifted down the narrow spiraling stairs, Forrest felt his heart begin to race. Rat trembled beside him. Together the two stood frozen in fear.

But it was neither a cry nor a scream that held their attention. For what came floating down the Bloody Tower's darkened stairwell on that early March morning was the loveliest, most haunting song Forrest Harper had ever heard.

XI
THE ENEMY

The chances of hearing a beautiful song within the clammy walls of the Bloody Tower were as rare as finding a rainbow in a hurricane. Forrest closed his eyes and listened.

"*Hush ye, my bairnie, bonnie, wee laddie . . . ,*" the voice echoed in the hollow darkness.

"I can't make out the words," Rat whispered beside him.

"It must be in that odd Scottish tongue, for 'tis coming from the prisoner's cell. 'Tis indeed a sad song she makes, that much I can tell."

With Tuck on his shoulder, Forrest climbed the last few steps up to the landing. He went to a door and peered through its small barred window. The strong scent of tallow and incense hung heavy in the close quarters. The incense was left over from the last prisoner to live there, the sad-faced Bishop, whose many prayers could not win him his freedom or his life.

The narrow cell was as damp and desolate as a cave. Its thick stone walls were blackened with soot, and the only furniture was an old oak table and chair. As his eyes adjusted to the darkness, Forrest watched the girl as she stood before the cell's only window. She was singing so sweetly, he dared not disturb her. Forrest couldn't help but notice how the long braid that hung down her back looked as if it had been spun of gold. He could have stood there and watched, listening to her beautiful voice forever, when Tuck decided to answer her song with one of his own. On hearing the raven's sudden sharp "*Kee*," the girl turned, her piercing blue eyes meeting Forrest's. Without a word, she backed into the shadows.

"Come with a drink and a crust, is all," Forrest said, and he turned the large key in the lock and pushed open the heavy door.

"If you fancy some rush for your floor, I can fetch some for you," he told her, as he set the mug and bread on the table.

The girl froze. Silent and stony-eyed, she watched as the boys traded uneasy looks.

"Well, you got a lovely fire going, anyway," Rat said. He walked up to the hearth and held out his hands to warm them.

"Father must have made it up," Forrest told him.

"This old Tower gets frightfully cold. Some rush on the floor would keep the dampness off a body."

He glanced at the girl, but she lowered her eyes and said nothing.

"As you like," Forrest shrugged, and he turned to leave.

"*Bide awee*," the girl called. "Wait a bit."

When Forrest turned back around, she had stepped out of the shadows. But Tuck stretched his neck in her direction, and she quickly backed away.

"He'll not hurt you," Forrest assured her. "He's quite tame. You needn't be afraid."

"I am not afraid!" the girl declared in a heavy Scottish accent.

Forrest tried to explain. "I thought you might be . . ."

"I know what you thought," the girl quickly interrupted in a tremulous voice. "I know what all you English think of me and my kinsmen. But you are wrong. 'Tis all a *wheen o'blethers*."

The boys looked blankly at each other.

"A pack of lies," the girl said impatiently. "For even here in your ugly English tower, we Stewarts will not be cowered."

Startled by this outburst, Forrest could think of no reply and quickly turned to leave.

"I've had nothing to eat or drink since yesterday

morn," the girl called after him. "Am I to have no more than beggar's bread?"

Forrest instantly regretted having stolen the sip of her tea.

"'Tis not for me to say," he said, turning back around. "I'm only to fetch you a mug and crust in the morning and empty your bucket. My father will bring you supper, but unless your family has paid for more, you best get used to beggar's bread."

A shadow crossed her face as she was once again reminded of the grimness of her situation.

Then, to Forrest's astonishment, Rat silently pulled the ginger biscuit from inside his shirt and held it out to the girl. She seemed as surprised by his generosity as Forrest, and an uneasy moment followed as she stared at the biscuit in Rat's filthy hand. Forrest realized that her hesitation might be due to the layer of filth covering Rat's fingers.

But the girl's hunger overcame her, and she reached out and grabbed the biscuit, gobbling it down hungrily. Tuck took to the air, flying over their heads.

"Do you not know 'tis bad luck to bring a raven under a roof?" the girl said.

"Some would say it is so," replied Forrest indignantly. "But only those who know nothing of ravens. I say 'tis far worse luck to have a babe under your roof."

"A baby?" Rat asked.

"Oh aye, they're far worse to have about the house than ravens," Forrest declared. He held out his arm and Tuck landed on his fist.

"My infant sister, Bea, why she can make a frightful roar that can wake the dead. And then there's her smell. At times, her smell is so bad she can set the candles a-quiver with it," Forrest added. "You'll not find a raven in all the land near as noisy nor as foul smelling as my baby sister, Bea," he declared.

Rat laughed, and Forrest felt his face flush on seeing the girl's curious stare. He immediately lowered his eyes, whereupon he found himself looking at the girl's hands. Though they were covered in dust from the road, Forrest could see that her fingers were delicately tapered, and on her thumb she wore a thin-banded gold ring set with a ruby stone. Forrest wondered who had given her such a ring.

"What of my father?" the girl spoke up. "Am I not to see him?"

"He is being held in another tower, here in the fortress. Other than that I have no news," Forrest told her. "Come, we best take our leave," he said, abruptly turning his back on the girl and motioning to Rat.

The two boys were heading down the steps when they stopped suddenly at the sound of the girl's voice calling after them from the grate of her cell door.

"Your raven. Has he a name?"

"Tuck," Forrest called up to her. "His name is Tuck."

Then he heard her voice echoing down to him, smooth and soft as a raven's wing. "Tuck, Tuck, Tuck."

Tuck turned back toward her, his ruff puffing out with approval.

As the boys continued down the steps, Forrest thought he heard the sound of crying.

"Maybe we should go back up," Rat suggested.

But Forrest shook his head no. He knew that it was not his place nor in his power to comfort her. For she was the enemy, the daughter of a Scottish Rebel. And he was an Englishman's son. And alas, they were in the Tower of London, a place where terror, not comfort, ruled the day.

XII
WITH THEIR HEADS COMING OFF

That evening the Harpers' candlelit cottage was filled with the strong aroma of sheep trotters and turnips. As Forrest set his bucket of coal down beside the hearth, he eyed the cast-iron pot hanging over the fire and smiled. Sheep trotters and turnips was one of his favorite meals.

Mary was curled up in their father's chair. She held a woolen bag against her cheek.

"What's wrong?" Forrest asked. "Your tooth again?"

Mary nodded. Forrest recognized the tooth bag that his mother always kept filled with salt and warmed when any of them had a toothache.

"It's been paining me all morning," Mary complained, as she put the bag down. But when she picked it back up, Forrest noticed that she had switched it to her other cheek.

"And which tooth is it this time?" he asked suspiciously, for Mary had a habit of having a toothache whenever she wanted to get out of doing her chores.

Mary made a face. "All of them," she said.

Forrest rolled his eyes.

"Will you tell me about your Scottish prisoner?" Mary asked, lifting the bag once more from her cheek.

"I've nothing to tell," Forrest said. He picked a piece of charcoal out of the ash bucket and slipped it into his pocket to use for drawing future battles on the shed wall.

"Oh, do tell me just one thing about her," Mary pestered, as she left the chair to swat a flitch of ham that hung beside the chimney.

"I've told you there is nothing to tell," Forrest said, exasperated, as he watched the ham spin in the air. "And leave that be or I shall tell Mother."

He pulled her hand off the ham and gave her a shove.

"*Telltale tit*," he heard Mary sing. "*Cut his throat a slit, and every little puppy dog shall have a little bit.*"

"Why must you be such a pest, Mary?" Forrest complained.

Hearing their voices, baby Bea gurgled from her cradle beside the hearth. Forrest took a cautious step toward her, sniffing the air as he went. Though she was smellier and noisier than his birds, Forrest thought Bea better company than Mary at times like these.

As he knelt beside the cradle, he couldn't resist tickling the pink folds of Bea's chubby neck to make her laugh. But as he did, the black soot from his fingers rubbed off on her white skin. Seeing what he'd done, Forrest couldn't resist running his finger along the baby's upper lip.

"Ahoy there, matey!" he cried. "We've got a pirate aboard this cradle, and I think she means to rob us all!"

"Oh, Mother will be in a temper when she sees how dirty you've gotten her," Mary cried, leaning over the cradle to look.

"Shhh . . . ," Forrest shushed her. "Where has she gone to, anyway?"

"She went to fetch some wool from Mistress Walker."

"Good," Forrest mumbled. He rubbed Bea's little chin black, giving her a perfect-looking goatee.

The mustachioed and bearded little Bea blinked her eyes and burped loudly as Forrest and Mary fell back laughing. Bea waved her hands and grinned. It was just at that moment that the cottage door opened and the Ravenmaster stepped inside.

"Father!" Forrest cried, jumping to his feet before the cradle. "You're home early."

"No earlier than usual," his father said wearily.

Beatrice cried from her cradle.

"Is that my little button of a Bea calling to her papa?" the Ravenmaster said with a smile. "Let me see my little angel," he demanded.

"Won't you let me help you with your bonnet first?" Mary insisted, rushing to his side.

While the Ravenmaster was busy removing his large velvet hat, Forrest scooped Bea into his arms and hurried over to the basin in the corner.

No sooner had he taken a wet cloth to her face than his mother walked through the door.

"Bless my soul, has she spit up on herself again?" Mistress Harper sighed. She set a basket of raw wool down on the sideboard. "I've never known a child so hard to keep clean."

"She was a bit of a mess," Forrest agreed, throwing the cloth back into the basin. "But I washed her up."

"You're a fine big brother, you are," his mother said with a smile.

Forrest saw Mary stifle a giggle, as he smiled back.

Mistress Harper turned to help her husband out of his heavy coat. "How goes it with you, sir?" she asked.

"As it should, my love, as it should," the Ravenmaster answered. "For no sooner am I in the door than our Mary here takes my bonnet, and in two shakes of a duck's whisker, she has it put away. Fine job, my girl. Fine job." He bent down to kiss the top of Mary's head and then turned to look at Forrest.

"Have you noticed our Will, how uppity he's been acting?" the Ravenmaster asked, as he settled into his chair at the table.

"Aye, he was strutting about this morning, fluffing out his feathers like the King at Coronation," Forrest replied.

"He'll be head bird one day, mark my words," his father said.

"But what shall happen to Thor?" Forrest asked.

"Oh, he'll be knocked down a peg or two," his father said. "Can't stay head bird forever. Much like men, birds are. Look at our own King George, with enemies itching to wear his crown. Just ask our new prisoner. She and her kinsmen would know about that. Which reminds me, did you fetch some rush for her floor?"

But Forrest didn't hear this last question, for he was too busy thinking about the King losing his crown and what the new prisoner had to do with that.

"Whatever are you daydreaming about now, lad?" his father asked, seeing the faraway look in his son's eyes.

"Perhaps he is dreaming about a girl," Mary teased.

"A girl?" The Ravenmaster's thick eyebrows lifted,

as he reached back to unbutton the stiff ruff collar from around his neck.

"The Scottish Rebel's daughter," Mary said, breaking into giggles.

Forrest felt his face burn red. "And you are as simple as an egg to talk such nonsense."

"For mercy's sake, Mary," their mother scolded, as she took Bea from Forrest's arms. "Must you always be looking to stir up a storm in a teacup?"

"Well, why will he not tell us about her?" Mary pouted.

"What shall I tell? She is a girl who likes to sing. That is all I know." He dared not admit to them how beautiful her voice was, nor how golden her braid.

"She sings then?" pestered Mary. "Of what does she sing?"

"How should I know?" Forrest shrugged. "For her words were not in English."

"Gaelic. 'Tis the language they speak," said the Ravenmaster.

" 'Twas a sad song," Forrest continued. "That much I could tell."

"Aye," the Ravenmaster said. "I can well believe it, considering the trouble she's found herself in."

"What is her crime, Father?" Mary asked.

"Treason," her father said simply. "Along with her

father and her uncle. They've all been accused of plotting against the Crown."

"Some say that the Scots are a nasty people, hardboiled and low-minded," Forrest said. "But can all Scots be that way, Father?"

"Blood is blood," the Ravenmaster replied. "There's no denying the bad traits carried in the blood. Be glad you're an Englishman, is what I say."

"And I've heard they are so fierce they foam at the mouth," Forrest continued.

"Foam at the mouth? Stuff and nonsense," his mother said, shaking her head. "Wherever did you hear such rubbish?"

Forrest shrugged. "There is talk going 'round the Tower."

"Best not believe all the talk you hear, my boy," she cautioned. "For people will say anything to inflame men's hearts in a time of war."

"There is no love in England for these Scots. That much is true. They're a treasonous bunch, the whole lot of them," his father added. "And those we are lucky enough to capture will surely be made an example of."

"But how?" Forrest asked.

"With their heads coming off," his father replied.

Forrest flinched at these words and quickly looked away.

"The sight of a Jacobite head atop a spike is the only way for the King to let the Scots know he means to put an end to their warring ways," his father said.

"Such things are not for us to decide," Forrest's mother interrupted. "The good Lord and our King will see a fit punishment is handed out. Mary, put the baby back in her cradle, and Forrest, fetch another candle for the table. Come, let us sit down to sup now," she said.

"Mmm, trotters," Master Harper murmured, as his wife placed a platter of steaming food upon the table.

"And there's bramble pudding for dessert," Mistress Harper said with a smile. "Forrest's favorite."

But bramble pudding was the furthest thing from Forrest's mind, for his thoughts had left the warm, cozy cottage. He was thinking instead of England's enemies and the bad blood running in their veins. And he thought of a cold darkened cell in the Bloody Tower and of the frightened girl who was locked away there.

Forrest felt a shudder pass over him as he recalled the hard edge of his father's words, "with their heads coming off."

XIII
A Girl Called Maddy

Forrest was on the path returning from the cages when he felt something hit him on the side of his head. It was as small as a stone and hard enough to leave a stinging sensation. He grabbed his head and turned just in time to miss a second missile come zooming through the air, straight for him.

"Good morn to you, little Hare Heart," Finch called from across the path. The bully had his slingshot out, and a boy beside him was handing him his next round of ammunition. The small balls of mud and dung had been perfectly shaped to fit his slingshot.

"How is that bloodthirsty prisoner of yours?" Finch taunted, as he aimed his weapon and pulled back the leather strap. Forrest ducked, but the mud ball caught him on the chin. He wanted desperately to run, or to turn around and go back but didn't dare to, for fear of them laughing even more. Instead he continued on as if nothing were wrong.

"The Constable must be so glad to know he has a warder big enough and brave enough to guard a little girl," the other boy laughed.

"Watch out that she doesn't attack you with one of her dolls," Finch whooped.

Remembering his father's advice, Forrest gritted his teeth and tried to ignore them. But try as he might, their comments stung more than the dung balls that flew about him, hitting him left and right. He quickened his step and began to run. The boys roared with laughter.

"Look at the little Hare Heart hop away," Finch cried.

As Forrest struggled to lift the shed's latch with his trembling hand, the mud balls splattered against the door. He rushed inside and slammed the door shut. Rat looked up from behind the bag of dead rats he was emptying into a bucket.

"Wot 'appened to you?" he asked, seeing Forrest's muddied shirt and face.

"Finch and some of the others ambushed me," Forrest said breathlessly, trying not to cry. "I can take a little mud, but 'tis the hateful names they call me that hurt the worst."

"Maybe they'll forget them once they find someone new to bully," Rat suggested.

"But I shall never forget," Forrest told him. "Some-day I will show them all that I am no Hare Heart!"

"Maybe this will help," Rat said, reaching into his pocket and handing him an old copper nail. "You can borrow my good-luck nail."

Forrest stared down at the old bent nail in his hand.

"It's brought me good fortune, and it may do the same for you." Rat smiled.

Forrest's dark brows knitted, as he fingered the nail in his hand. "What's the good of some old nail?" he quipped. "That won't help anything."

Rat's happy face crumpled before him. And Forrest felt bad for having said what he did. A short silence followed.

"Who told you this was a lucky nail?" Forrest finally asked. He was surprised to see Rat blush.

"No one 'ad to tell me," Rat said, lowering his eyes to the floor. "I just knew it."

"How? How did you know?"

"I knew it was lucky, on account of Tuck gave it to me on the first day you spoke to me," Rat said softly. "That made it lucky, you see."

Forrest felt a guilty tug at his heart and slipped the nail into his pocket.

❧   ❧   ❧

Later that morning, Forrest climbed back up the many steps to the Bloody Tower. The lucky nail was in his pocket as Tuck flew overhead.

When he reached the prisoner's cell, Forrest looked in through the grate to see the girl on her knees, praying. He wondered what God thought when he heard the prisoner's prayers. Did God know that she was the enemy?

The girl quickly got to her feet and smoothed down her skirt. Her large blue eyes were ringed with circles. He knew that she must have slept little, if at all. It was always the same with the new prisoners. The terror of finding themselves in the Tower was enough to keep most wide awake with worry.

"What news of my father? Have you any news of him?" she pleaded through the bars of her cell.

"Nay," Forrest answered.

And as he fit the key into the lock, he couldn't help wishing that her father was his prisoner instead of her. Then Finch and the others might show him some respect.

Once inside the cell, he set the mug and bread on the table and removed the waste bucket. He left without saying a word.

This routine was repeated for several days in a row.

The girl remained totally silent, except for a bad cough she had developed.

" 'Tis the dampness and the dark of the place that sickens them," Forrest had heard his parents saying about the prisoners at supper. His father had mentioned the names of the prisoners who had taken sick and died in their cells. The list was long.

Forrest couldn't bear to think of the girl becoming sick and dying. In fact, it bothered him so much that he began to sneak extra food from home for her breakfast. He brought a fig one day, an oatcake another. He placed them on her plate so that she wouldn't know that he had gone out of his way for her.

The next morning, when Forrest left his cottage, a hard, damp wind blew from off the river. He heard the loud snapping of the flags atop the White Tower and shivered as an icy drizzle began to fall. As he climbed the many steps in the frigid, dark stairwell, his only thought was to warm his cold hands by the fire in the girl's cell.

But when he unlocked her door and stepped inside, the chamber was as chilled as the stairwell. The prisoner was huddled by the icy hearth and wrapped in her cape, her teeth chattering loudly between coughs. The fire in the grate was nearly out.

It was then that Forrest understood just how wealthy her family must have been, for the prisoners who were least able to take care of themselves were usually those accustomed to having servants wait on them. A simple task, such as keeping a fire alive, was something they had had no need to learn.

"You've piled too much coal on the grate," Forrest declared, when he saw all of the unburned coal. Then he brought in the iron poker that was kept outside the door. Within minutes, he had laid a new fire. It wasn't long before the twigs began to crackle and burn.

"You must add only a little bit of coal at a time," he said with his back to the girl. He tossed a small shovelful on the fire.

"I didn't know," she admitted.

Forrest hadn't heard her speak since their second meeting, and he didn't know what to say. But Tuck did. The little raven hopped off Forrest's shoulder onto the floor. He lowered his head and spread his neck feathers, and he rasped his familiar greeting.

Forrest was amazed. "Tuck has never given that greeting to anyone but me and Rat," he said. "He is not very friendly with strangers."

"In the Glen, I had a *wee hoolit* who would come feed from my hand," the girl said. Before Forrest could stop her, she reached out to stroke Tuck's head feathers. Once again, he marveled at the raven's friendliness, for Tuck never let strangers pet him.

"*Wee hoolit*?" Forrest asked.

"A baby owl," she told him, as she warmed her hands before the fire.

While the two talked, Tuck flew up to the girl's mug and dipped in his beak.

The girl smiled, and Forrest smiled back. For just a moment the world seemed to slip away, and they were neither Scottish nor English, neither prisoner nor guard, but simply two children enjoying the company of a raven.

"You're awfully impudent, Tuck," Forrest scolded, as the raven flew to the window. "Why, the young miss will think I've taught you no manners."

"My name is Madeline McKay Stewart," the girl said. "But I am called Maddy."

An awkward silence followed.

"What is your name?" she whispered.

"Forrest," he told her. "Forrest Harper."

"Can you tell me any news of my father, Forrest?" Maddy asked.

He thought about what his father had said, how the Rebels had committed treason and were a threat to

England and how they would be made an example of, but he didn't have the heart to tell her, so he just shook his head no.

They both grew quiet again until a loud scratching noise sounded from the corner of the room. The twitching whiskers of a large black rat squeezed out of a chink in the wall. Forrest kicked the wall with his boot, but the rat had already disappeared back into the hole. The color had drained from Maddy's face.

"I will try to bring the rat catcher tomorrow," Forrest promised. But no sooner had he said it, than he wished he hadn't, for it would be wrong of him to try to give her special treatment. He was already sneaking up extra food to her. He had to remember that she was a Scot and a Jacobite's daughter.

Maddy smiled shyly, and he saw her deep blue eyes watching him. But he quickly looked away, for he didn't want her to see his confusion.

She is an enemy to England, he told himself. He should hate her with all his heart. But how? How was he to hate this girl who talked so gently to Tuck? How could he hate this girl who fed baby owls? How was he to hate this girl called Maddy?

XIV
A Boy Called Ned and a Bonnie Glen

The next day, Forrest returned to Maddy's cell with a bundle of rush on his back and Rat following close behind. Forrest was relieved to see that Maddy's cough had grown no worse.

"Come on, Barnabas, out you come," Rat whispered into the rat hole.

"Barnabas?" Forrest repeated.

"I always call the fat ones Barnabas, after me Master," Rat said, as he stuck a small, clove oil–soaked rag into the hole. "Though he'd take his switch to me backside if he knew."

The three grew quiet as they waited for the rat to appear.

"Your name," Maddy finally spoke up. " 'Tis a good name for a rat catcher but not a proper name for a boy."

Rat shrugged. "Master Meeks give me that name when I started working for him. Ain't been called anything else for years."

"But what is your real name?" Maddy asked.

Rat ducked his head in embarrassment. "Ned," he whispered shyly. "My name is Ned White."

Forrest said nothing as he unloaded the bundle of rush from his back. He was too surprised to speak. He felt bad for all the time that he'd known his friend and had never thought to ask him his real name.

"I would have called you by your true name if I had known you had one," he finally said. "'Tis a good name, Ned." Saying his name felt awkward to Forrest, after having called him Rat for so long.

"'Tis a fine, proper name," Maddy agreed.

Ned blushed.

Suddenly, a loud scratching sound came from the mouse hole, and the little rat catcher spun around.

"Gotcha, Barnabas!" he yelped, as he threw his bag over the rat.

Ned's little oval face brightened as he tied the bag tight.

"I'm much obliged to you," Maddy told him. "For I thought I should go *gyte* with worry, that he'd come out of his hole and bite me while I slept."

"*Gyte* with worry?" Ned repeated.

"Aye," Maddy said shaking her head. "Or, I suppose you English would say, 'crazed with worry.'"

The children were silent for a while. Then Forrest

asked, "How is it that you have come to know our language?"

"My nurse, Flora, taught me," Maddy explained, as she straightened the hem of her skirts. "Her mother was English. She came to live with us after my mother died, and she never really learned to speak Gaelic properly. My grandfather could not bear to hear me speak English, but my nurse and I could have wonderful secret conversations. And each night, she would listen to my prayers and together we'd say one in English as well, though I never told Grandfather."

"Your mention of night reminds me that I mean to leave you these," Forrest said, as he handed her the bundle of rush he'd brought for her. "The Tower's stones make a cold bed to lie on."

"In truth, I've slept on many a chilly bed these last weeks," Maddy admitted. She grew silent then, as her eyes moved about the dark, damp cell to the heavy oak door that stood ajar. Forrest could see a hopeful spark come into her eyes.

"You best put any thoughts of escape out of your mind," he told her, as he motioned for Ned to close the door. "Even if you could get past the sentries at the entrance, you'd get no farther than the first portcullis. The regiment soldiers are everywhere, and I promise you the Tower guards are most determined. Whether in skirts or breeches, you will be hunted down and torture will be your only reward."

Maddy lowered her eyes and twisted the end of her braid about her fingers as the boys finished spreading the rush over the floor.

"When you spoke of sleeping on many a chilly bed these last weeks, can you tell us where those places were and what they were like?" Forrest asked, hoping to hear all about her adventures.

The color rose in Maddy's cheeks, and her golden eyebrows knit over the deep blue of her eyes. "Is that why you've shown me such kindness? You're spies, then!"

"We are not spies," Forrest told her. "But I would gladly be one if my King should ask it of me." He thrust out his chest. "For I am loyal to my country and no traitor."

Maddy's lip quivered, as she met his defiant gaze. "And I am no traitor to my home, to my Scotland," she said in a trembling voice.

"I've never seen Scotland," Forrest said, mesmerized by the very sound of the word.

"Have you never been beyond London?" Maddy asked in disgust.

Forrest squirmed uneasily, then he shook his head no. "I've never slept anywhere but within the Tower's walls," he admitted.

"You've never slept anywhere but in the shadow of this gloom-filled Tower?" Maddy asked. "How frightful!"

"'Tisn't as bad as all that, really," Forrest insisted, petting Tuck, who was on his shoulder. "For the armory is full of armor and crossbows and all manner of weapons. And the moat, when it doesn't stink too badly, makes a good pool to float leaf boats on or play at Ducks and Drakes. And there are always soldiers coming and going. Though I would surely love to leave with them one day so that I might prove my courage and see the world."

"A funny thing it is," Maddy said. "You long to leave your home, and I long to return to mine."

"And I've never 'ad a 'ome of me own to know," Ned said wistfully.

Maddy's eyes filled with sympathy.

"Wot's it like? Your home?" Ned asked her.

Her face brightened. "Aberdeenshire in Glen Gairn? Why the Glen is as bonnie a place as God ever created." She leaned back against the cell's stone wall and closed her eyes.

"There is the sweet scent of the heather on the moor behind our house," she smiled, and her face relaxed as she called up memories of her home. "And the burn is filled with speckled trout. And my little twin brothers, Gavin and Owen, whoop and holler as they try to chase a toad over the stones. Then there's the heron that skims the crystal waters of our loch where my cousin Ella saw a fairy once."

The boys sighed deeply as she continued.

"And you can hear Roddy McDougal's pipes in the moonlight and see the moor all covered in frost as a herd of red deer cross it. And in summer there's the clean, lovely smell of a white Scottish rose and the sight of a tattie-bogle knee-deep in buttercups. Oh, I can see it all so clear."

"Hallo! Are you up there, lad?" the Ravenmaster's voice echoed up to them from below.

Forrest blinked, as if waking from a dream. He looked at Maddy, who had opened her eyes. He didn't want her to stop. If only he could hear Roddy McDougal's pipes or know what a "tattie-bogle" was.

But the voice from below reminded Forrest that they were not in the glen in Aberdeenshire nor in a field of buttercups but rather in a damp, dark cell, deep within England's largest and most heavily guarded fortress. And Forrest Harper suddenly remembered the chores he still had to do, the cages to clean, and the ravens to tend to.

XV
The Fourth Shadow

That night, lightning flashed over the battlements and rain pelted the Tower's turrets. But Forrest did not even hear the storm that wheeled in from the ocean and broke over London's rooftops. For he was curled under his coverlet, sound asleep and dreaming. And in his dreams he saw a boy wearing a blue cap, running through a field, golden with buttercups. Forrest heard the boy's laughter, saw the glint of sunlight in his green eyes, and heard the beating of his heart.

"Free!" The boy laughed. "So free!"

Forrest awoke to the sound of rain against the roof. He closed his eyes and tried to imagine Ned lying down in the depths of Barnabas Meeks's cellar. Could Ned hear the rain way down there? And what of Maddy, alone and cold up in the Bloody Tower? Was she listening to the rain and remembering what it sounded like as it fell in her glen?

The dank weather did not let up as rain continued to fall all morning. It splashed the Tower's black cannon clean, licked the moss from its many stone walls, and turned its battlements into slippery catwalks. Forrest was careful to dodge the puddles as he made his way to the ravens' cages with a bundle of fresh straw on his back. Because he owned only one pair of boots, keeping them dry was of the utmost importance. He'd have to suffer through the day with wet, cold feet if he didn't.

He was glad the downpour had let up and there were only puddles and a misty drizzle to contend with. He tried to cheer himself with thoughts of the next battle he planned to draw with Ned. Forrest decided it should be the battle Henry VIII fought against the French. His father had told him all about the brave King Henry and how he had fought the French more than two hundred years ago.

Forrest was going over the battle in his head as he pulled a handful of old straw from Thor's cage.

"*Kee, kek, kek,*" the head bird scolded, as he watched from the ground.

"I don't know why you always complain when I change your straw," Forrest told him. "I wish I had someone making up a new bed for me now and then. Mother hates to climb up the ladder so 'tis left to me to do for myself."

But the huge raven ruffled his neck feathers and

complained louder. Forrest was about to go on to the next cage, when he looked over the low stone wall and saw the stooped figure of Simon Frick in the distance, heading toward the White Tower. Forrest shuddered at the sight of the four ragged little shadows trailing the sweep. He was about to turn back to his work when something nagged at him.

Hadn't there been only three children with the sweep the last time they had met?

Forrest walked to the wall to get a closer look. The frightful little group following Frick was so covered in ash that it was difficult to tell each little sweep apart. But there was something familiar about the fourth child's walk. His legs were not nearly as blackened as the others, and his clothes not nearly so shredded. Forrest squinted through the mist as the gentle rain washed the ash from the little one's cap to reveal its true color of blue.

"Ned!" Forrest gasped. He could hardly believe his eyes. It really was Ned. But how did that evil spider, Simon Frick, manage to catch him in his web? Forrest climbed over the low wall and took off after the shadowy group, hiding behind trees so the sweep wouldn't see him.

"Wait here, all of you," Simon Frick hissed when they reached the outer stairs of the White Tower. "I won't be long."

The little figures nodded like zombies, their big red-rimmed eyes as vacant as the painted eyes on Mary's peg doll. Only Ned looked alive as he lowered a bag of soot from his shoulder and turned his head to search the Green.

"Ned," Forrest called, running up to him. "Oh, Ned, what's happened?"

Ned's lip began to tremble so badly on seeing his friend, Forrest could barely make out the words that poured out of him.

"Master Meeks had too much ale last night at the tavern. He got into a card game with Master Frick and started losing badly. Master Meeks lost a right lot of money, he did. To make good on his word, he used my indenture to pay off his debt. He sold me, Forrest! Sold me to the sweep!"

"You've got to get out of here," Forrest gasped, as he glanced at the three motionless children beside them.

"The only way to do that," Ned replied, his eyes filling with tears, "is to repay the money to the sweep. But if I cannot, Master Meeks told me I am to shut my mouth and do as I am told. I begged him then, told him I'd do anything he asked, anything at all, jest as long as he wouldn't sell me to Master Frick."

"What did he say to that?" Forrest asked.

Ned swallowed hard. "He shoved me down and told

me I was an ungrateful boy after all the good he'd done me. And I'm to serve out the rest of me years climbing for Master Frick."

Forrest eyed the closed door at the top of the stairs and then looked up to see the thin curls of smoke pouring out of the Tower's chimneys. He pulled Ned close, so the others could not hear. "You must run away," he whispered. "You must!"

Ned's little chest heaved as he sucked in a sob. "Where would I run to? I don't know a soul in the city. Ain't got a ha'penny to me name. Couldn't even buy me a crust of bread, much less lodgin's. And the Sweep said if I tried to run away, why he'd hunt me down and slit me throat with his own knife. Said no boy ever lived who tried to run out on 'is indenture." His voice lowered to a frightened whisper. "And I do believe him for he's that evil, he is."

Forrest nodded, not doubting Ned for a minute. "If we could only find a way to pay him off."

"Where am I to get five pounds?" Ned said miserably, as his tears streaked his soot-covered cheeks. "Might as well be five hundred pounds. Or five thousand."

Forrest knew he was right, for like Ned, he never saw any money of his own except for the occasional halfpenny his mother gave him to buy a ginger beer from the girl who wheeled her cart down Water Lane.

He wished now he had saved all those halfpence. And even more he wished he had some encouraging words to offer.

"I don't know how I can help you," he whispered, trying not to cry himself. "But I know I won't give up. I'll be back soon, Ned. I promise I will."

Forrest heard the door of the White Tower creak open, and he darted away down the path. He was reeling from the hideous sight of those children covered with soot and bruises and the horrible stench that surrounded them.

Yes, those children are worse than dead, Forrest decided. And he couldn't let that happen to Ned. He just couldn't.

He ran and ran until he could run no more. When he finally stopped to catch his breath, he found himself before the great doors of the armory. He pulled his slingshot out of his pocket. Somehow, just holding it made him feel better. He searched the ground for a good stone.

When he saw two warders coming out of the armory doors, he decided to step inside. His eyes traveled over the hundreds of swords, lances, daggers, and muskets displayed on the walls. The gleaming steel was laid out with such precision in such intricate patterns and designs, the sight of it always left him breathless.

The sheer might of the Crown and the magnitude of its strength was overwhelming. Forrest thought about all the men who had held those weapons and the strength and courage they must have had, and the promises they must have been able to keep.

How can I be like them? Forrest wondered. For he knew that if he were to keep his promise to Ned, he would have to find the courage to be strong. If only he could be a man wielding one of those swords or lances, instead of just a boy with a slingshot and a stone.

XVI
PROMISES

The next morning, the stairwell of the Bloody Tower felt as dark and silent as a tomb. And as Forrest trudged up to Maddy's cell with Tuck on his shoulder, he thought of Ned and the deadly darkness of the chimneys he'd be forced to climb. But when he heard Maddy's voice echoing down from her cell, he stopped to listen. Perhaps her songs helped to brighten the gloom of the darkness that surrounded her.

When he reached her cell, Forrest was surprised to see a candle's flame flickering on the table. And though Maddy was back on her knees, she was not praying. This time she was drawing! Using a piece of charcoal from the grate, she covered the entire floor of her cell with designs.

"I've come with a mug," Forrest said quietly, so as not to startle her as he unlocked the cell door. "And how have you come by the candle?"

"It was a gift," Maddy told him. "A priest who is a

friend to our family paid me a visit and made a gift of two candles. I am ever grateful."

Forrest stepped inside, then knelt beside the girl to get a closer look at her drawings. "Many have left their marks on the Tower walls," he said, as his eyes traveled over the designs. "Though I fear your marks will not last as long as those that have been scratched into the stones with steel."

"I have no wish to leave my mark in this foul place," Maddy whispered.

"Then you do it for amusement?"

"I do it to ward off evil," she said haughtily.

"You draw well," he told her. "Who taught you?"

"My nurse Flora taught me to chalk a doorstep with the image of a rowan berry. Flora is old and wise and some say she has got second sight."

"Second sight?"

"Aye, she can see spirits and fairies and sometimes the future. Flora said I would need the rowan to protect me on my journey. The rowan tree has powerful magic against evil," she whispered, tracing her finger around a design. "And there is much evil in your devilish country."

Forrest bristled at the remark. Did she think all English people were evil? It was then that he remembered how the English always spoke of the Scots as savage, low-minded people, who foamed at the mouth. Looking at Maddy, Forrest realized how silly these stories were. For her manner was so graceful and her eyes so bright, no one could ever call her savage or low-minded.

"Not *all* Englishmen keep company with the devil," he said, reaching into his pocket and pulling out the oatcake his mother had given him that morning.

Maddy blushed as he placed it on the table.

"Forgive me," she said. "I am not ungrateful for the kindness you've shown me."

Forrest shrugged uneasily at her mention of kindness, for it was not his intention to look for compliments. "I do have something I would like to ask you," he said. "Yesterday you spoke of hearing pipes in the moonlight. I was wondering about those pipes. Are they not played in church by candlelight as our pipes are?"

Maddy smiled. "*Ach,* no! 'Tis not an organ's pipes, but bagpipes, the kind held in a piper's arm. And they are loud so they must be played in the open air. They would be grating on your ear under a roof. But from a distance, under the sky, the sound of them goes straight to your heart. A Highlander cannot help but be filled with pride when he hears them.

" 'Tis why they are played to call the clans to arms

and to take them into battle, for nothing will stir the blood of a Highlander like the sound of the pipes. 'Tis why the English want to outlaw them from our lands."

"Do you think they will outlaw them?" Forrest asked.

Maddy frowned. "There is talk of it. And talk as well of your English King forbidding our men to carry arms or wear the kilt. Why, my grandfather has carried his dirk since he was a boy. He says he will die fighting for the right to carry it, rather than live unarmed. And as for your breeches, only a Lowlander would be unmanly enough to wear them. Your English kings have tried to rob us of our ways for centuries, and this one from the House of Hanover is no different. He gives us no choice but to fight."

Her blue eyes suddenly flashed with anger, and Forrest felt an uncomfortable chill between them. Once again it took Tuck to lighten the mood, for he suddenly flew from the window's ledge and startled them both by landing on Maddy's arm.

"Why, hallo, Tuck," she gasped. Tuck lowered his head and murmured a greeting. Then he walked down her arm and cocked his head, giving the ring on her finger a quizzical look. He tried to peck it, but Maddy quickly covered it with her other hand.

"He loves anything that shines," Forrest told her.

"He'll pick up any shiny object he can find and carry it back to his nest in his beak."

"You're a bonnie fellow, aye, you are," Maddy whispered in a voice so soft and sweet, Forrest smiled. He understood why Tuck trusted her so. But when the raven stretched his neck, trying next to peck at the pouch at Maddy's waist, both she and Forrest began to laugh.

"Now he's making a pest of himself," Forrest told her.

"'Tis fellows like you who cause the farmers to put out their tattie-bogles," Maddy said, as she coaxed him onto her hand.

"What's that?" Forrest asked.

"Tattie-bogles are the straw folk that farmers set in their fields. Put there to scare the crows off the oats," Maddy explained. "My brothers Gavin and Owen are afraid of them. They've not yet turned three, you see. Owen even has nightmares about them. He wakes Gavin and soon they're both crying in their beds, and they won't stop 'til I sing them my song." She closed her eyes and began to sing,

"Hush ye, my bairnie, bonnie, wee laddie,
When you're a man you shall follow your daddie. . . ."

Her voice trailed off as she opened her tear-filled eyes.

"That is the song you were singing before," Forrest said. "What does the Gaelic mean?"

" 'Hush, my baby, my beautiful little boy,' " Maddie told him. " 'Tis a song I imagine my mother would have sung to them. And when I sing it, I imagine myself home, not here, not in the stink of this dark tower but rather home in our bright, beautiful Glen with the scent of the earth and flowers everywhere. And my brothers are beside me, and my father is with us as well. And the fighting has stopped, and the English soldiers are far to the south, and the only thing to fear is some harmless tattie-bogle out in the field. When I sing, I'm there."

Forrest knew just what she meant, for with his spyglass, he often imagined himself far from the Tower. Tuck meanwhile had gone back to pecking at Maddy's pouch.

"I don't suppose a tattie-bogle would frighten Tuck much," Forrest said, reaching for his raven. "He's too cheeky to be fooled by a straw man."

"I had a fine pet once in the Glen," Maddy said, her tears betraying her smile. "She was a little red fawn and very smart. She tried to follow us when the soldiers came to take us away, but we rode so fast, she couldn't keep up."

Maddie began to cry, and Forrest looked away. "I am sorry. We do not have to talk if it upsets you."

"Nay, I'm glad for your company," Maddy told him, as she wiped the tears from her eyes. "I'm a Stewart. We're a strong people, you see. I've no business wetting my cheeks. We don't give in to weakness. I know I will leave here one day and return to my little brothers in the Glen."

"Who is caring for them now?"

Maddy frowned. "They're staying with my Auntie, but she has lost her husband and son in the fighting. Her heart is weary, and her health is frail. It will be up to me to raise them when I go home." She paused. "*Dree yer ain wierd*," she whispered in Gaelic. "'Tis a saying we have. Look here, inside my ring." She removed the ruby ring from her thumb and showed him the words inscribed around the inside of the gold band.

"But what does it mean?" Forrest asked.

"Face up to your destiny," Maddy told him, as she slipped the ring back onto her thumb.

"Destiny?"

"Yes, it means the things that are fated to happen to you," Maddy explained. "Good things and bad things. It takes courage to face all we are meant to live through."

"And what about you?" Forrest suddenly blurted out. "Were you meant to commit treason? Was it your destiny to plot against our King?"

"But I did no such thing!" Maddy exclaimed. "My

father and uncles have been fighting for the land we've lived on for generations. The Redcoats had come to burn down our house. They arrested us for trying to put out the fire and called it treason. They claimed we were trying to thwart the Crown's intent."

"But they cannot take your life for that," Forrest cried. "Did you tell the Tower's Constable what happened? They cannot punish you for a crime you did not commit. 'Twould be unjust!"

Maddy turned her face away from him. "When it comes to our people, the English court knows no justice. When it comes to Scotland, your King is only interested in ridding the land of our kind. But he will have a fight on his hands, for our soldiers are not like his cowardly Redcoats."

"What are they like, the Highland soldiers?" Forrest asked.

Maddy turned and looked him in the eye. "They are the bravest, strongest, most noble soldiers to ever do battle," she said proudly. "Their loyalty to Bonnie Prince Charlie never wavers. With broadsword and dirk, they'll defend him. Every Highlander lives for the day the Prince can take his rightful place on the throne in Edinburgh."

Forrest lowered his eyes, for he knew such talk was treasonous.

"My father is of noble blood," Maddy continued. "He has fought in many battles to see our lands restored. But for all that, he never once missed helping me to collect the first May dew." Maddy smiled. "'Tis a custom we have in our hills. If a girl washes her face in the first dew of May, 'tis said her skin will glow and her beauty will shine. Mothers usually take their daughters out to collect the dew, but since my own Mother is dead, Father has gone in her place, even though he insists my beauty needs no help." She blushed.

As he looked at her pale, soft skin against the gold of her hair, Forrest couldn't help agreeing with her father, though he didn't dare to say so.

"In truth, I look forward to those first days of May all year. For only then do I seem to have my father all to myself, without his clansmen discussing battles or my brothers wanting to ride on his back."

"He must be very brave, fighting all those battles," Forrest said. "Has he killed very many men?"

Maddy nodded. "But 'tisn't the killing that makes him brave. My grandfather always said my father has a pure heart. There's no cunning or guile come with him, and he loves as fierce as some would hate. Grand-father said that when you walk the earth with a pure heart, you've naught to fear. 'Tis love that gives you courage, not hate."

Forrest watched Maddy as she lifted the edge of her skirt and worked some stitches loose along the hem. She removed a little twig and quickly pulled the stitches closed and tied a knot.

"My love for my father gives me the courage to beg this favor of you," she whispered, as she placed the twig in Forrest's hand. "If you will promise to see that my father gets this bit of rowan, I will make it worth your while."

Forrest examined the tiny twig. "What is it for?" he asked.

" 'Tis a charm," she answered. "It contains the magic to keep away harm. My nurse would not let me leave the Glen until she had sewn it into my hem. I beg of you," she whispered, "see that my father gets it. I worry so for him."

"But . . . but I cannot do such a thing," Forrest stammered. "For it is forbidden to pass things between prisoners without permission from the Constable."

"How could anyone object to such a small token?" Maddy pleaded. "And if you do that for me, I will give you this in return."

To Forrest's amazement she took the ruby ring from her thumb and handed it to him. Never had he held anything so precious before. "Where did you get this?" he whispered.

A shadow crossed her face. " 'Twas my mother's ring. She wore it until the day she died."

"And you would part with it so easily?" Forrest asked.

"In truth, it tears my heart in two," she told him. "But if it means protecting my father, I would part with all I owned."

Forrest looked back down at the ring and thought about his own father and the love he had for him.

" 'Tis worth much gold," Maddy whispered.

"Five pounds worth?" Forrest asked.

"That and much more," Maddy assured him. "And you may have it all if you would only see that my father gets the twig."

"Your father is in the Bell Tower," Forrest whispered. "And like you, he is held close. 'Twould be easier if he had the liberty to leave his cell. If the warders were to see me give it to him, they'd arrest me for certain."

He looked up at Maddy's pleading eyes and then stared down at the ring. "I don't want to take your ring from you. But Ned is in grave trouble," he whispered. "He's been sold to the Tower sweep and will be made to climb chimneys till his indenture is paid off. If he had five pounds he could pay off the sweep and be free."

"Then you *must* take the ring," Maddy told him,

"whether you take the charm to my father or not. You must use the ring to help Ned."

Surprised by the kindness of her offer, Forrest slipped the ring into his pocket. "I will take it," he whispered. "And I will see that your charm reaches your father as well." He slipped the twig in his other pocket.

Maddy's face brightened as if the sun itself had come out. She whispered something in Gaelic, then she reached for the sprig of white heather that was tucked into the sash around her waist.

"And this is for you," she said, pressing it into his hand. "It's good luck."

As he went about the rest of his chores that day, Forrest's thoughts were full of luck and love and hate and courage. He thought of the Scottish Rebels who were fighting for the customs and the land they loved. He thought of the English people who knew so little of them and yet were ready to fill their hearts with so much hate, enough hate to punish an innocent girl. And he thought of Ned and the luck he needed so badly.

Once he was alone in the shed, Forrest turned the ring over and over in his fingers. As he did, he read the words inscribed on the band.

"*Dree yer ain wierd.* Face your destiny," he said aloud.

What is Maddy Stewart's destiny? he wondered. *And what of Ned's?*

As he thought of the promises he'd made, he wondered if keeping them was to be his destiny.

"*Dree yer ain wierd,*" he whispered under his breath, and he hid the ring in the bottom of his pocket.

XVII
IN THE SHADOW OF THE AXE

By nightfall, the storm over London had worn itself out, and a silvery sliver of moon hung over the Tower's glistening turrets. The Harpers had finished their evening meal and had taken their places before the fire.

The Ravenmaster sat in his chair, reading his paper. The smoke from his clay pipe swirled in the still air. Mistress Harper nestled beside him with her sewing as she gently rocked baby Beatrice's cradle with one foot. Nubbins meowed loudly as Mary tried to give her peg doll a ride on his back.

Meanwhile, Forrest sat on the bottom rung of the ladder at the foot of the loft, silently whittling a small forked branch of wood for a new slingshot. His heart pounded as he stopped every now and then to feel for the rowan twig in his pocket. He looked at his parents and wondered what they would do if they knew what he was hiding. It felt strange to be keeping so many secrets from them. But he couldn't tell them about his friendship with Ned or Maddy or about his plans to go to the

Bell Tower that very night to deliver Maddy's charm to her father.

Anxiously, he left the ladder and headed across the room, where he silently picked a walnut out of the bowl on the sideboard and tiptoed to the door.

"And where do you fancy you're taking yourself?" his mother asked.

"Nowhere," Forrest replied casually. "I was just going to take Tuck for a little walk."

"You're in the company of that bird all day. Surely that's enough." His mother frowned. "Besides, there's fever going 'round and one must take precautions. 'Tis safer indoors, I do believe. The apothecary from Chancery Lane has promised to bring me a bottle of milkweed physick tomorrow. He guarantees it will clean out the innards and ward off the pox."

"But, Mother, you've had us swallowing more physick than food this winter," groaned Forrest.

"And you've had little complaint of ill humors because of it," she reminded him.

"I am only going for a short walk. I won't catch the pox on the way, I promise," Forrest pleaded.

"I see no reason to be going out after dark and falling in with riffraff," she said, shaking her head.

"Oh, do let the lad alone, Bess," Master Harper intervened. "There's no harm in his taking a stroll.

You'd think we were living in the city, for mercy's sake. 'Tisn't Thieves Alley he'll be walking in, but Tower Green." He winked at Forrest and nodded for him to go.

"Stay and play with me and my poppet," Mary begged, pulling on his sleeve.

"Not now, Mary," Forrest said, wiggling out of her grasp.

"And do stay away from the moat," his mother called after him, as he lifted the wooden latch and slammed the door shut.

Forrest loved to be out at night. He loved leaving the closeness of the cottage. What adventures could he have in that smoky room, with his mother hovering over him with bottles of physick and his sister pushing her poppets in his face? In their company, he was just Forrest, an eleven-year-old boy, but at night, out on his own, he felt older and bigger and braver. Still, would he be brave enough to get into the Rebel Scot's cell and hand him the twig? He prayed all the way to the shed that he would.

Once there, he opened the door and whistled two long whistles. Within seconds, the flapping of wings echoed into the night, and soon he and Tuck were on their way to Bell Tower.

Never in his life had he done such a thing as

passing keepsakes between two prisoners. He felt Tuck's beak nuzzling his neck, and it gave him the courage to go on. Forrest quickened his step. He knew much would depend on who was on sentry duty that night at the Bell Tower. As they approached the entrance, Forrest squinted at the two tall figures standing guard in the flickering torchlight. From a distance, the uniformed warders in their high, broad-brimmed bonnets and crimson coats all looked alike. Forrest took a step closer.

"Who goes there?" a deep voice called out, while a white-gloved hand gripped a partizan.

Forrest sighed with relief for he recognized the voice at once. It was Warder Bothy and that meant that Warder Finch was on duty with him.

"'Tis only me, Master Bothy," Forrest answered. "Forrest Harper, out for a stroll."

"Oh, aye!" the voice instantly relaxed into a friendly tone. "Well, come closer, lad, for we almost mistook you for a spy."

Forrest clutched the twig in his pocket so tightly he almost broke it in two.

"I'm no spy," he croaked.

"'Tis fortunate for you, you're not," Warder Bothy replied. "For we most always catch 'um. And when we do, we string 'um up smart or take off their heads if they be noble. Like that prisoner of yours, the little Scottish wench."

"But she hasn't even been tried yet," Forrest reminded him.

"If the King is out of patience, he'll do away with a trial and pass sentence himself," Warder Bothy replied.

"Best way to deal with traitors, before they get a foothold and bring down the country," Warder Finch added. "Show them no mercy is wot I say."

"She's just a girl," Forrest pointed out. "What harm can she do?"

"They teach treason in the cradle, them dirty Scots do," Warder Finch replied. "And the Tyburn Jig can be danced at any age, I reckon."

Forrest knew that when prisoners were hung at Tyburn and their arms and legs jerked about as the rope tightened around their necks, they were said to dance the Tyburn Jig.

"And what of our clever raven friend here?" Master Bothy asked, turning to Tuck. "Taught him any new tricks?"

Forrest nodded. "Though I'll need a coin to show you," he said.

"Oh, aye?" Warder Bothy winked at his fellow warder, as he dug a halfpenny out of his pocket. " 'Twill cost us, will it?"

"Take the coin and throw it high," Forrest instructed. No sooner had the warder thrown the coin above his head, than Tuck flew up and snatched it in midair.

Forrest whistled a long whistle, and Tuck dropped the halfpenny into his hand, mimicking the whistle note for note.

"That's jolly good." Warder Finch grinned.

"Someday, I shall teach him to speak," Forrest bragged.

The warders cheered and clapped as Tuck glided down to land on Forrest's shoulder. Forrest knew that the boredom accompanying long hours of sentry duty often left the warders starved for any diversion. A clever raven was well worth the cost of a few pence. He watched as they dug into their pockets for more coins.

"I expect our new prisoners would pay for a show as well, if they were here long enough to enjoy it," Warder Bothy said.

"So it is the new Jacobite prisoners you're guarding?" Forrest asked, trying hard not to seem too interested.

"Oh, aye, but not for long, I reckon," replied Warder Bothy.

"Why? Are they to be moved?" Forrest asked.

"They are to be moved all right," the warder told him. "They and the little wench you're guarding will be moved by barge from Traitor's Gate to Westminster tomorrow morn."

"They're to be tried that soon?"

"Tried on Thursday and executed by Friday, if the Crown had its way," Warder Finch said. "Word is, the King plans to make an example of them. His vengeance will be swift, no doubt."

Forrest felt his stomach lurch.

"Do you really think they'll execute them?" he asked. "Even my prisoner?"

Warder Finch shrugged. "She sleeps in the shadow of the axe, if she sleeps at all. She's highborn, so the Crown will spare her the noose and take off her head."

" 'Twill roll with the rest of 'um," Bothy added. "She best pray for John Wilcox to have a steady hand on the day she's to meet him."

Forrest felt the hairs on his neck stand up at the mention of John Wilcox, the Executioner. He knew that only those of noble blood died by the axe rather than by the rope. His head was suddenly spinning. Maddy and her father were in the gravest danger. And Forrest feared it would take more than a twig of rowan to save them now.

XVIII
THE GO-BETWEEN

"Aye, the coffin maker will be a busy man once we catch all these Rebel Scots," Warder Bothy said.

"Why even waste good English wood on their coffins?" Warder Finch snorted. "Traitors and devils, the lot of 'um. Better to just burn them all is wot I say." He turned to Forrest. "How about that little she devil you're guarding? Has she given you much trouble?"

"Nay, not much," Forrest answered, as he dug his hand into his pocket and felt for the twig and sprig of heather hidden there. "Is Master Haines standing guard at the Scots' door tonight?" he asked. "I promised to bring Tuck to see him."

"Nay," Warder Finch replied. "The new man, Tittle, is on duty. He's a decent sort but a bit nervous. 'Twill seem a long night for him, I warrant."

"Always is for those new to the job," Warder Bothy added.

"Do you suppose the new warder would care to see some of Tuck's tricks?" Forrest offered.

"Looking to squeeze a few pence out of him, hey?"
Warder Bothy grinned. "Well, truth be told, I should
think he'd fancy a bit of a show. Come along then, lad,
and I'll take a walk up with you."

Warder Bothy reached for a torch from the iron
hoop on the wall. Forrest and Tuck followed him into
the Tower and up a darkened stairwell. The musty
smell of mold growing on damp stony walls hung in
the air.

They were greeted by a white-faced warder at the
top of the landing.

"I say, Bothy! You gave me a scare, you did," the
rattled warder cried. "Thought you were Anne Boleyn's
ghost, as I stand here."

"Don't talk rubbish, man," Warder Bothy snorted.

"Aye, 'tis nonsense I'm sure," Warder Tittle said
sheepishly. "Being new to the Tower, my nerves are a
bit jangled, I suppose."

"Surely that's it," Bothy assured him. "Besides,
every warder here knows that Anne Boleyn's ghost
prefers the Lieutenant's Lodgings."

The warder winked. Forrest knew full well how the
warders liked to tease those new to the Tower.

As the men talked, Forrest looked at the door
behind them. Through a small grate, he could see that
the room was unlit. Suddenly, in the glow of the

warder's torch, a man's ringed hand appeared at the bars. It was the ring that caught Forrest's eye, for it was a gold band set with a ruby stone, identical to the one Maddy wore.

"Come now, Tittle, how'd you fancy hearing a raven whistle?" Master Bothy was saying.

Forrest had to force his attention away from the hand at the grate, the hand that he knew must belong to Maddy's father. He whistled, and Tuck instantly whistled back to him. Then he tried to get Tuck to whistle again, but the raven had grown tired of the game, and before Forrest could stop him, he flew over their heads.

As the two warders were busy calling out to Tuck and trying to coax him down, Forrest inched closer to the cell door. He tried to make out the face behind the bars, but it was too dark to see.

"I'll wager I can get him to whistle for me," Warder Bothy boasted.

"A shilling says he won't," Warder Tittle countered.

And soon, each was shouting and gesturing for Tuck's attention as they followed him to the landing.

Forrest knew that his chance had come. If he was going to pass the twig, it would have to be now. But it was as if his hands had suddenly turned to stone and his feet were rooted to the spot. He couldn't move.

But when he thought of Ned climbing up the Tower's dark and dangerous chimneys and maybe never coming down again, he managed to pull the rowan twig out of his pocket. And standing on tiptoe, he passed it through the barred window. "'Tis from Maddy," he whispered.

He was about to move away when he heard the faintest reply.

"Be you friend or foe to the Jacobite Cause?"

Forrest felt his mouth go dry as his eyes darted back to the warders. They were still occupied with Tuck.

"I'm friend to Maddy Stewart," he whispered beside the door.

The ringed hand passed a small rolled paper through the bars.

"For her eyes only," the man whispered.

Forrest's heart was racing. With a trembling hand he reached for the paper and silently slipped it into his shirt. And with that one gesture he crossed a line he had never intended to cross. For now Forrest Harper had left the confines of English law to become a conspirator in keeping with accused traitors to the Crown. The Ravenmaster's son was now a go-between for the Scottish Rebels!

XIX
FOR HER EYES ONLY

The curfew bell sounded in the night. From a prisoner's lonely, dank cell, the sound of the bell was a somber reminder of another day's freedom lost. But to the warders and their families living within the stone walls of the fortress, the ring of the bell offered a comforting sound as they snuffed out their candles and took to their beds. While the penny papers were filled with stories of thieves roaming the city willing to kill for a pair of candlesticks or a coverlet off a bed, it was reassuring to know that the Tower gates were locked fast.

But on this night the ringing of the bell brought Forrest little comfort. He lay awake in his bed, unable to sleep. Maddy's ring gave him hope to buy Ned's freedom. But his worries for Maddy grew with the passing night. As he closed his eyes, he heard Warder Finch's words echoing in his mind: "She sleeps in the shadow of the axe, if she sleeps at all."

Forrest thought of Maddy's bluebell eyes. It pained him to imagine those eyes closed forever. He thought about Tom Knight, the Highwayman, and his ignoble end at Tower Hill. Jeered and spat upon by the crowds, Maddy's final moments would become no more than a spectacle and amusement for the city.

She didn't belong riding in a cart, jeered and spat upon. She didn't belong buried under the earth or burned to ashes but rather living in her Glen, in her bonnie Glen Gairn, with a *wee hoolit* at her hand and buttercups at her feet. After hours of worrying, Forrest closed his eyes and fell into a fitful sleep.

When he awoke the next morning to the familiar crowing of the neighbor's cock, he smelled the stink of tallow and lye.

"Wash day," he groaned, as he pulled the quilt over his head.

Forrest hated wash days. He knew that, besides doing his regular chores, he and Mary would be enlisted to help. This meant fetching buckets of water from the well, carrying in extra buckets of coal for the fire, and standing over a hot cauldron, turning a boiling, foul smelling mixture of brown suds and sweat-stained cloth. He also knew his mother would be short of temper, since she and Mary had to wake hours before dawn to begin the demanding task of washing the entire family's clothes and bed linens by hand.

My breeches! Forrest thought frantically. He owned only two pairs of trousers, and his mother always insisted Mary bring them down on wash days. In the pockets of his dirty pair were the sprig of heather, the ring, the note for Maddy, and Ned's good-luck nail. Where were his trousers? Did his mother already wash them?

He sprung from his bed, found them on the floor where he'd left them and rushed to empty the pockets. He pulled out the note and the crumpled sprig of heather, but Ned's lucky nail and the ring were missing! Quickly he pulled the other pocket inside out, only to find a large hole in it.

"The nail!" he gasped, realizing that it must have torn a hole in his pocket, a hole big enough for the ring to slip out. He got down on his hands and knees and searched the floor, but there was no sign of the ring.

Forrest closed his eyes as he took another breath of the acrid air. How could he have been so careless with something so precious?

There was nothing to do but get dressed.

Carefully, Forrest checked the pockets of his clean trousers to be sure there were no holes in them before slipping the note and the heather deep inside. He hurried down the ladder from the loft in his stocking feet and almost slipped and fell on the worn footholds.

"What's this, then?" His mother looked up from the pot of bubbling foam she was stirring. "I've never known you to be so eager to set about your chores on a wash-day morning."

Forrest sat down beside his stiffened boots at the hearth and began working them open. His eyes were glued to the floor, as he searched for the ring.

"Whatever are you looking for?" his mother asked.

Forrest quickly picked up a stray piece of charcoal and held it up to the firelight. "This will be good for drawing with," he told her.

"Be sure your chores are done before you use it," his father said, as he sipped his tea at the table. "You'll need to get an early start today. Take the young Miss her mug first thing, for the barge will be at Traitor's Gate within the hour to carry her and her kinsmen to Westminster."

"And after their trial, what then?" Forrest asked.

"Only God and the King know the answer to that," his father replied.

As Forrest reached for a mug from the sideboard he longed to ask for advice.

"What if the girl is innocent, Father?" he asked. "What if she never committed the crime she is accused of? Who should protect her?"

His father sighed. "She very well could be a victim of circumstance, considering the family she comes from, but 'tis a time of war, lad. Protecting the innocent is a luxury rarely indulged in by warring peoples."

Seeing the look of horror on Forrest's face, he set down his mug on the table. "War isn't kind *or* fair. But she is a Scot," he said firmly. "And she will breed more Scots. Her menfolk have sworn allegiance to our foes. If the King decides they must pay with their necks, there's an end of it."

Forrest struggled to hold his tongue, but he knew that once his father said, "there's an end of it," the conversation was over. There would be no more discussion. He laced up his boots and then bolted for the door. All the way to the shed, he kept his eyes peeled to the ground, praying that he'd spot the ring.

Once at the shed, he whistled for Tuck. "We've got to get to the Bloody Tower. There's no time to waste," he whispered.

When they finally reached Maddy's cell, Forrest found her curled up under her cape, asleep on the floor. She stirred when she heard the door open and sprang up at the sound of his voice.

"My charm," Maddy whispered anxiously. "Were you able to get it to my father?"

"Aye, he has it."

"Oh, God be praised," Maddy exclaimed. "And Ned? Were you able to get the ring to him?"

Forrest's back stiffened. "No, not yet," he told her. He didn't have the heart to admit that he had lost it.

With a loud sigh, Maddy sank into the chair beside the table. As Forrest looked on, he couldn't help thinking how small she seemed there in the big chair, so small and fragile, like a little bird in need of protection.

"What is it?" she asked. "Why do you stare at me so?"

"You are to travel to Westminster within the hour," he told her. He could see the fear in her eyes. "Before you go, I must tell you this." He took a deep breath and stepped closer to the table. And the words came tumbling out before he could take them back.

"I believe you are innocent. So whatever happens, you can count on my friendship."

Startled by this sudden pledge, she stared back at him.

"My father says that war is not fair," Forrest continued. "And yet all my life he's taught me the importance of fairness in a man's character. Why is it that when people grow older, they say one thing yet do another?"

Maddy sighed. "Sometimes I think it would be a better world if we didn't have to grow up. Then there would surely be no war."

Forrest thought of all the battles he and Ned had drawn on the shed wall. "Or maybe they'd just be fought with charcoal on a wall," he said.

"You've been a good friend to me," Maddy told him, reaching for his arm.

"I wish there was more I could do to help you."

"There are other friends, friends of my father. They, too, wish to help," she said.

"Good," Forrest said, as he gave her a halfhearted smile. But even as he did, his heart was pounding in his chest.

What did she mean about her father's friends? Who were they? And how were they to help? What was she trying to tell him?

There were so many questions and so little time for answers. Maddy's life was hanging by the thinnest of threads. Forrest knew just how dangerous his pledge of friendship to her was and that what he was about to do next could put his own life in the gravest danger. He took a deep breath, plucked the note from his pocket, and placed it in her trembling hands.

XX
OUT OF LUCK

Forrest stepped back outside into the crisp morning air. With Tuck flying just ahead of him, he made his way through the Inner Ward where the mist rose off the frost-tipped grass of Tower Green. He stopped before the pretty Lieutenant's Lodgings on the Green and watched the smoke pour from its chimneys.

His heart sank at the sight of it, as it reminded him of Ned and the horrid chimneys he must be climbing.

Later that day, it was all he could do to keep his mind on his chores. As he carried water from the well, he tripped over Mistress Walker's pig that had gotten loose. Water went flying! The pig squealed! Mistress Walker screeched! And warders hooted with laughter.

Fetching coal for the fire proved no better. Forrest absentmindedly dumped a scuttle full of coal into the chamber pot his mother had just scrubbed clean and left outside the door to dry.

Later that afternoon, he almost set himself on fire as he took his turn stirring the wash.

"Whatever are you daydreaming about now?" his mother cried, as the smell of singed breeches hung in the air.

But Forrest stood silent, unable to answer.

"In truth, you're more a danger than a help to me today," she sighed. "You best go out to the cages with your father. At least there you won't be setting yourself on fire."

Forrest found the Ravenmaster busy at work, rebuilding a cage door.

"Hold this wire here while I nail it into place," his father ordered. "Our Odin is anxious for me to finish. And Henry will not leave his side."

As Forrest held the wire, he turned his head to see the two ravens watching intently from a few feet away.

"'Tis quite something how those two do look out for each other," Forrest's father remarked. "You usually see that kind of closeness in birds who have mated. But what we have here with Odin and Henry is true friendship. Ever since they were fledglings it's been so. And even though Henry is the smaller bird, he'd fight those much larger to protect Odin."

"Why do you suppose they are so close?" Forrest asked.

His father shrugged. "'Tis their destiny to be friends, I suppose."

Forrest wondered if it had been his destiny to meet Ned and Maddy. But what kind of friend could he be to either of them now?

" 'Tis not always easy to be a good friend, is it, Father?" Forrest asked.

"No, I suppose not," his father replied.

"But then how does Henry do it? How does he have the courage to face the bigger birds?"

His father hesitated. "Sometimes," he said, "your love for someone is bigger than your fears. Courage comes from that kind of love, I suppose."

"But how do you know if you have that kind of love for someone? Enough love to be that brave?" Forrest asked.

"Well, you cannot always know until the time comes when you are tested," his father told him. "Sometimes the need to right a wrong is so great, 'tis almost as if you have no choice left. You feel it in your very bones. And you can do nothing else but follow your heart."

They finished the cage door in silence. Tuck flew down to inspect the job, and Master Harper held out his arm to him.

" 'Tis time we heard a few words from you, is it not, Master Tuck?" he coaxed. "Can you say, 'Tuck? Tuck? Tuck?' "

"I practice talking with him every day," Forrest

complained. "But he has yet to say a word. I cannot tell if he is being stubborn or if he just cannot do it."

His father smiled. "Could be a bit of both. I've taught only one bird to speak in all my years as Ravenmaster. But Tuck is quite clever. And you've done a good job with him. Keep practicing and be patient. He very well could be the one bird who speaks for you. But now we'd best get over to Water Lane to try to find the woodsman. We'll need some oak boards to replace the floors of these old cages."

They set off together down the path, and when they reached Water Lane, another warder called out to them.

"Ho there, Master Harper." He waved them over. "Have you heard the news about your prisoner and her kinsmen?"

"No, John," the Ravenmaster called back. "What news?"

"The Rebel Scots tried to escape as the barge reached Westminster," the warder told them, as he came closer. "Jumped into the river and tried to swim for their lives."

Forrest's heart skipped a beat.

"God bless the Crown and our warder's good aim," the man continued. "The Scots were shot dead, and their bodies fished out. You'll likely see their heads on the Hill by nightfall."

The warder's cold, steely voice worked like an icy dagger in Forrest's chest. He struggled for breath.

"Were all three killed?" Forrest managed to ask. "Even our prisoner?"

"The little Jacobite wench?" the warder snorted. "Why do you ask, lad? Could it be the little Scottish hussy has turned your head?" He winked at Forrest's father.

Forrest felt his face reddening, but said nothing more.

"Your prisoner lives," the warder told him. "They were able to hold her back before she could jump. She continued on to Westminster for her trial. Though she probably wishes she had jumped with her kinsmen and ended her miseries then and there."

Forrest sickened at the thought of Maddy having to endure the murder of her father before her very eyes.

"I wonder how many other traitors' heads we'll see on spikes now that March has come and the weather is warming," Forrest barely heard the warder say.

"Aye," the Ravenmaster agreed. "I dare say those Scottish dogs have been lying in wait, what with all the snow we've had this winter."

Forrest couldn't think about the snows of an English winter. His thoughts, instead, had turned to the first dew of a Scottish May and a motherless girl whose heart had been so full of love for her father. How broken must that heart be now?

Meanwhile, as the warder walked on, Forrest heard his own father say, "Ah, well, bad business, that, and the poor little wench to live through it all. Well, we can do naught but keep busy and do our work." He started down the Lane.

"But what is to happen to her now?" Forrest asked, walking beside him.

"She'll go on trial, and the Crown will see justice done," his father said with a weary sigh. "Though in truth, I think enough punishment has been done, her having gone through all she has."

"Will they let her go back to her home in Scotland?"

His father shrugged. " 'Tis hard to say what they'll judge fair."

"And what if the King denies her a trial?" Forrest asked. "What then?"

"When his Majesty deems it necessary, he does away with a trial and most often the prisoner's days can be numbered on his hand, unless he lets them linger. In that case, he can have their heads taken off whenever he chooses, now or ten years from now. 'Tis the King's will."

"But how can we be sure she'll receive justice,

Father?" Forrest said hotly. "What if they've wrongly accused her?"

"Still your tongue, lad!" His father shot him a harsh look. "Such talk is treasonous. 'Tis not our place to decide the guilt or innocence of any prisoner. 'Tis up to the Crown. Our job is to see his Majesty's will done and no more. If the King wants the wench's head, he shall have it. But until that time, we'll do all in our power to keep watch over her here in the Tower, and there's an end of it."

Forrest pushed his hands into his pockets and stared down at the ground. And as he wrapped his fingers around the sprig of heather in his pocket, he recalled Maddy's words, "for luck."

But what if her luck had run out? Her father and uncle were dead. And now her own life hung from a delicate thread as she waited to stand before her accusers. Forrest gripped the crumbling heather in his pocket so tightly, it snapped in two.

XXI
THE STRANGER

As Forrest accompanied his father down Water Lane, they stopped at the woodsman's wagon.

"Have you any oak?" the Ravenmaster asked. He rifled through the boards that were piled in the cart.

The woodsman shook his head no and offered to bring some to the Tower the following day. The Ravenmaster asked about the price, and, as the two men talked, Forrest pulled his spyglass from its case. He held it to his eye and tried to see Maddy, not in England, but in her homeland, in her Glen. He had just focused on a shimmering lake when he heard a familiar voice call, "Ah, Ravenmaster, I've been meaning to speak with you."

Forrest looked up from his glass to see Master Meeks standing before them.

"We've missed your rats," the Ravenmaster told him. "I've had to buy horse meat instead for my birds."

"Lost me boy to the Tower's sweep in a game of whist," the old rat catcher confessed. "But I'll be getting another soon enough. In the meantime, I'll try to stop by your shed with a day's catch when I 'av a chance." He gave a nod to Forrest. "Seen your boy with them birds. He certainly 'as a way with 'um."

The Ravenmaster looked at Forrest and smiled.

"Handles them better than I do," he boasted. "He'll be a fine Ravenmaster himself one day."

Forrest blushed with pride. But he had little time to enjoy his father's praise, for the sight of Simon Frick approaching caused him to catch his breath.

"Fine breeze today, hey, Ravenmaster?" the sweep called out in his rasping whisper. "Keeps the stink of the moat from our noses."

"Aye, it does that," the Ravenmaster agreed.

But Forrest could tell from the cold tone of his father's voice that he had no wish to make conversation with Simon Frick. Master Meeks showed an equal disdain for him as he muttered something under his breath and spat onto the ground.

"And a bad win your little rat turned out to be," the sweep said, turning to Master Meeks with a scowl. The old rat catcher just glared back at him. Forrest held his breath at the mention of Ned.

"I can't use 'im at all. He's no good to me until the bleeding stops and his skin scabs over," Simon Frick continued.

"He's hurt?" Forrest blurted out.

"Oh aye, 'is delicate skin is all scraped up and burned, especially 'is knees and 'is elbows. Until his skin heals 'ee's no use to me."

Forrest ached at the thought of Ned hurt and bleeding. And the thought that he had been so close to saving him from such a fate was almost too much for him to bear.

As the sweep and the old rat catcher walked off together, the Ravenmaster turned to Forrest and whispered, "Stay away from that one, do you hear? His heart is as black as the chimneys he sweeps. I don't trust him. I don't trust him at all."

"Aye, Father." Forrest nodded. "But what about the rat catcher's boy? What will his life be like now?"

"Most likely it will be shorter, considering the dangerous work he's to do. Who can say if he'll live long enough to live out his indenture."

"But where does he sleep?" Forrest asked.

"I couldn't say what hole that black-hearted sweep keeps his climbing boys in. Some hovel in the city, close to the Tower, no doubt."

But his father had other things on his mind. "Pity the woodsman hasn't the oak we need today," he grumbled. "We'll try again tomorrow. You best go on back now and get the birds fed. There's horse meat in the shed."

Sometime later, as the ravens flocked around Forrest's feet and Tuck perched on his shoulder, he reached into a bucket and pulled out a chunk of horse meat.

"*Kee . . . kee . . . kee*," Tuck called.

"Yes, I know," Forrest said. "You're hungry, too."

He reached into the bucket, pulled out a piece of meat and fed it to Tuck.

Meanwhile, two of the other birds fluffed their feathers and nipped at Forrest's boots.

"All right, you two, you're next," Forrest said, throwing them each a chunk of meat. As he watched them eat, he couldn't stop thinking of Ned.

How badly hurt was he? Where was he staying? And when would he come back to the Tower?

While he had no answers to such questions, Forrest's only comfort was in knowing that at least Ned would not be forced to climb again until his skin healed. Forrest hoped he'd be safe wherever he was.

As he threw a chunk of meat to the birds, he noticed a workman who had stopped beside the cages. From the bundle of tools the man carried on his back and the dusting of sawdust in his red beard, Forrest could see that he was a carpenter.

"I'll wager your ravens eat better than most beggars," the carpenter remarked.

Forrest shrugged as he reached for the heavy leather glove in his back pocket and placed it on his hand. He took another hunk of horse meat and held it out to Thor, who was waiting at his feet.

"Caring for such special charges must be quite a task," the carpenter continued. "You must have learned much from your father. You are the Ravenmaster's son, are you not?"

Forrest gave the man a questioning stare. "Aye," he finally replied. "I am."

The carpenter took a step closer. "And have you a sprig of white heather given you for luck?" he whispered.

Forrest bristled. "Who are you?"

The man's eyes swept over the area. "I will need to see it before I would speak further," he said mysteriously.

Forrest reached into his pocket and pulled out the broken sprig of heather Maddy had given him. The muscles in the man's face relaxed on seeing it. He pulled a piece of meat from Forrest's bucket.

"Act as if nothing unusual is happening," the man commanded. He threw a piece of meat down to Thor. "I am just a carpenter, stopping to have a look at the ravens."

"But you are not really a carpenter, are you?" Forrest whispered. "Even though you sound English, you're one of them. You're a Jacobite Rebel. You're one of the friends Maddy spoke of."

"Who I am is not important," the man told him. He threw another piece of meat to the birds. "The important thing now is to know who you are."

"What do you mean?" Forrest asked.

"Is it true that you are a friend to the daughter of Owen Stewart?" the man whispered.

Forrest felt his heart racing but said nothing.

"A good enough friend to save her life?"

"What are you saying?" Forrest asked anxiously. "The trial, is it . . . ?"

"The trial has been denied," the man cut him off. "I've just come from Westminster. The King has passed judgment. Madeline is to die by the axe in a fortnight."

A wave of nausea swept over Forrest.

"Unless," the man whispered, "she is able to escape."

"Escape?" Forrest gasped.

"Maddy will be returned to the Tower," the man told him. "Because you work here, you will not be under suspicion. Everyone knows you, and you can move about freely. And because you are just a boy, no one will suspect you. You are in the best position to save Madeline Stewart's life."

Forrest's thoughts raced with dizzying speed.

"Take the night to think about it," the man whispered. He pressed a gold coin into Forrest's hand. "There are nine more of these should you decide to help us."

Forrest stared at the coin.

"Until the morrow," the man said, turning away.

"But where?" Forrest cried. "When? How will I find you?"

"You needn't worry," the man told him. "I shall find you."

XXII
THE REBEL HAS HIS ANSWER

Forrest spent a restless night, tossing and turning in his bed. As the hours passed and the dawn grew closer, his restlessness turned to panic. The Rebel Scot said he would find Forrest. And he would want an answer when he did. But Forrest had none to give.

To help Maddy, he would have to commit treason, putting himself at the greatest risk. Everyone working at the Tower knew that any escape would be thoroughly investigated. Anyone found involved would be rooted out, hunted down, and brought to his knees before the Constable of the Tower, who answered only to the King. Punishment would be swift and merciless.

Forrest thought of his family then and how they would suffer if he were found out. He imagined the shame he would bring on his father and the sorrow his mother would bear. He imagined his sister Mary's heartbreak if her brother were made to dance the Tyburn Jig.

He wondered how he would dare to take such a risk.

♊ ♊ ♊

"Look there. 'Tis Hare Heart," a voice called through the fog the next morning, as Forrest walked to the Tower with Maddy's breakfast.

Forrest stepped forward and found Finch and one of his friends blocking his way. But Forrest's thoughts were so preoccupied with matters of life and death that the bullies seemed a small threat by comparison.

"Get out of my way. I haven't time for you two now," he answered impatiently. Finch blinked in surprise.

"What was that?" the bully demanded angrily as he and his big-muscled friend stepped closer. "Were you speaking to us, Hare Heart?"

But Forrest simply ignored their taunts as he pushed through them and kept on walking. The boys were so taken aback by his lack of fear that they let him pass. And though he was glad that he had stood up to them, it seemed a small victory now compared to the dangers he faced.

When Forrest reached the Bloody Tower, he found it was just another workday for those working at the Crown's fortress. Warders went about their business tending to their prisoners as though all was well with the world.

Forrest listened to the deadly silence as he and Tuck made their way up the Tower's steps with Maddy's breakfast. The silence seemed louder and sadder than any sound Forrest had ever heard.

When he reached her cell, he found Maddy sitting in a corner, staring blankly as a huge river rat boldly ate the cheese off a plate on the table.

Forrest put the key into the lock and pushed the door open. The rat, hearing the door's loud creak, turned its head, then ran down the leg of the table, carrying the cheese between its pointed, sharp teeth. Maddy didn't budge as it slowly loped past her, stopping only to look up at Forrest before scurrying out the door.

"Maddy!" Forrest cried, as he rushed to the table. "Did you not see the rat? What is wrong with you?"

But she stared straight ahead, her face the color of the stones of the White Tower. "There's so much ugliness in this world," she mumbled. "So many rats."

"It could have bitten you," Forrest said.

She smiled faintly. "My father is murdered and your King will soon have my head. Do you really think I fear the bite of a rat?"

"You must look after yourself," he told her.

She closed her eyes and sighed. "I have nothing to live for now."

"But you do. You do." Forrest took her by the shoulders and shook her. "You must think of your brothers if not of yourself. You must stay alive for them, for Gavin and Owen."

She seemed to stir out of her stupor on hearing her brothers' names.

"If only I could," she whispered. "But your King will see me dead afore I can ever see their sweet faces again."

"Unless you were to escape," Forrest told her. And he suddenly knew that he could not live with himself unless he did something to help her. It was just as his father said. He could feel it in his bones.

The sound of footsteps echoed from outside the door and Forrest was startled to see a gray-headed priest shuffle into the cell.

"The guards gave me leave to visit with the prisoner," the priest said.

Forrest stared at his face, for there was something strangely familiar about the man, though he could not say what. He gave Forrest a long look.

"It is all right. He is a friend," Maddy told the man.

The priest placed his hand on Forrest's shoulder.

"A good friend, I hope," he said.

The statement hung in the air as Forrest tried to place the familiar voice.

He knew that he had known him from somewhere. But his hair was red, not gray, the last time he'd seen him.

"You are the stranger who stopped me yesterday, aren't you?" Forrest whispered.

"Aye, 'twas me," the man replied. "Have you made your decision to aid us, then? We've so little time. If we are to succeed we must act tonight."

"Tonight?" Forrest repeated anxiously. "So soon?"

The man nodded. "We dare not tarry. We must act now." He turned to Maddy. "God willing, you will not suffer another night in this damp cell. I promised your father that if any harm were to come to him, I would see you and your brothers safe. I mean to keep that promise."

"But how?" Maddy asked.

"There will be a boat waiting at the King's Stairs tonight," he told her.

Forrest could hardly catch his breath. They were plotting an escape, and he was to be part of it.

"Go through the Sally Port and over the Sally Port Drawbridge. It is the best way out, for it bypasses the gates and the main drawbridges," the man continued. "The boat will be at the King's Stairs at half past nine." He paused, giving Maddy an almost tender look as he held her wrist.

"You must be strong and stay calm for your life will depend upon it."

Maddy bit down on her lip and nodded.

"A woman has been hired to pose as a Stewart relative, to come to the Tower to pray with you," the man continued. "She's to come late this afternoon. With her will be a servant girl. Once in the cell, the servant girl will trade clothes with you, and, God willing, you will be able to walk out of here unrecognized. The woman will direct you to a shed on Water Lane where you'll wait until it's time to go to the boat."

"But what of my father?" Forrest interrupted. "For he brings Maddy her evening meal. If he discovers she is gone, he will alert the Tower guards."

"That is how you shall earn your gold," the man said, turning to Forrest. "You must arrange to bring the meal instead of your father."

"I could try," Forrest replied.

The man's dark eyes flashed. And Forrest could see his temples bulging.

"To try is not good enough!" He spat out the words as he grabbed hold of Forrest's shirt and drew him close. "You must do more than try. You must do it. Lives will depend upon it. Do you understand?"

"Aye." Forrest gulped. "I understand. But what of the other warders? You aren't planning to harm them, are you?"

"We're only interested in seeing the girl to safety tonight. If all goes well, no harm will be done to any.

But we must take care how we go about it." The man released his hold on Forrest's shirt. "Bide your time. Wait for the right moment to suggest to your father that you fetch the meal. You must give him no cause to suspect anything out of the ordinary."

"I will be questioned afterward," Forrest pointed out.

"Your answer shall be that the prisoner was asleep with her cape over her and you thought it best not to wake her. Do you understand?"

"Aye," Forrest said.

"Good," the man replied. "Now, we best leave before the guards suspect something." He turned to Maddy and kissed her hand.

"God willing, by nightfall you will be on your way home to your brothers," he whispered, "and sailing away from this English nightmare."

"Bless you," Maddy whispered back. She reached for Forrest's hand next. "God bless you as well, Forrest. You have shown me great kindness. I only wish I can show you the same one day."

As Forrest looked into her bluebell eyes, he felt his heart breaking. For he knew that if all went well, he would most likely never see Maddy again. He would never hear her songs or listen to her stories about the Glen. He wondered how much darker the old fortress would seem without the brightness of her smile.

He wanted to tell her this and so much more, but "good luck to you" was all he could manage. He blushed as she gave his hand a squeeze.

Once outside the cell, Forrest put the key into the lock and headed for the steps when the man pulled out a small leather pouch from under his robes.

"Hide it in your shirt, where no one will see," he ordered.

"What is it?" Forrest whispered, as he slipped the pouch into his shirt.

"It is the payment promised you."

Forrest had been so concerned about helping Maddy that he had forgotten about the gold.

"Just take care to live up to your part of the bargain," the man said, as he started down the steps.

"The escape," Forrest whispered after him. "Do you believe it shall work?"

"I cannot say," the man replied. "But God help us all if it should not."

XXIII
A Dirty Lie

Forrest had never held so much money in his hand before. He went right to the shed with the gold, fearful that he might lose it.

No sooner had he opened the pouch and pulled out some coins, than Tuck flew down from the rafter, and landed on Forrest's shoulder, anxious to inspect the shiny objects.

"Never thought we'd see the likes of these, hey, Tuck?" Forrest whispered. Tuck murmured as if in agreement and nudged a coin with his beak.

"Oh no," Forrest said, pulling it away from him. "You'll not get one of these. They're not tin. They're gold, Tuck. Real gold!"

He was putting the coins back into the pouch when he had the ominous feeling that they were not alone. His eyes darted around the dark shed, and the hairs on the back of his neck stood up as a shadow moved in the corner. He quickly hid the pouch back in his shirt. He could feel Tuck's heart beating in his ear as the raven fluffed out his throat hackles in alarm.

"Hey!" came a hoarse whisper.

Forrest jumped and let out a cry, but he drew in a sigh of relief when he saw Ned looking out from behind a barrel.

His face was blackened with soot, and his hat and hair were covered in ashes. As he stepped out into the light, Forrest felt his stomach twist at the sight of Ned's badly burned and bloodied knees.

"Ned?" he whispered.

"Aye," Ned said. " 'Tis me."

"But what are you doing here?" whispered Forrest.

"I've run away," Ned told him. "And I ain't goin' back. I'll take me chances in the open air, rather than go up one o' them chimneys again. Let him come after me if he wants to," he said wearily. "I'd rather die by the knife than by burnin'."

Forrest put his hands on Ned's bony shoulders.

"But, Ned, you don't have to go back up," Forrest told him, the excitement rising in his voice. He pulled out the pouch and emptied it onto the worktable. "You can use these to pay off your indenture." He picked up one of the coins and handed it to him. "You'll be free, Ned. You'll be free."

"'Ave mercy on me soul!" Ned gasped. "Where'd they come from? Did you rob the Tower's mint to get them?"

Forrest quickly explained how Maddy had offered her ring and how he had lost it. He also told Ned of how the Scot paid Forrest in gold to help Maddy escape.

"There's enough here for you to pay off your indenture and to get lodgings and food in the city besides." Forrest grinned.

Ned blinked, too stunned with his good fortune to speak. "Am I dreamin'?" he finally asked.

"No," said Forrest. "It's no dream. We'll go and pay off the sweep together."

"But where will we say the gold come from?"

Forrest scratched his head. "We'll say we found it beside a wagon. He could think what he likes. Maybe it was a wagon from the mint or a cart carrying some nobleman's belongings to his cell. I can't go with you until I finish my work. You can hide in here until then."

All day long, Forrest was distracted with thoughts of what lay ahead and was unable to hide his jittery nerves.

"Confound it, Forrest, do hold that wire still or your thumb will end up under my hammer!" his father fumed later that afternoon. The two were back at the cages repairing doors. "Whatever is the matter with you, boy? You're as fidgety as a hen about to go under the axe."

"Sorry, Father," Forrest muttered. "I was just thinking."

"Thinking?" his father echoed. "Have mercy on my soul, I'm not raising a philosopher. The only thoughts in your head should be on your work. Now, hold that wire still."

Forrest did as he was told, and his father nailed the wire into place.

"Ach," Master Harper groaned, as he rubbed his back.

"What is it, Father?"

"'Tis nothing one of your mother's mustard plasters won't cure," his father replied. "I'll have her mix me one up tonight. 'Twill draw out the ache in my back, to be sure."

Forrest took a deep breath and tried to steady his voice.

"I could bring the prisoner her sup, if you like," he offered. "'Twould do your back good not to have to climb all those steps."

His father smiled. "Ah, now there is the sort of thinking I approve of."

Forrest's heart pounded. The plan was in motion. And if everything went as it should, Maddy would not be there to eat her supper.

While Forrest fed the birds, Ned hid behind a barrel in the shed. But it wasn't long before Ned grew restless and began to draw on the wall with the piece of charcoal he carried in his pocket. He drew a dragon's body and was so consumed by his picture that he didn't hear the shed door open. And he didn't hear the footsteps until they were right behind him.

"Forrest, is that . . . ," Ned began.

But his words were cut short by the cold, spindly hand that clutched his neck and the gritty fingernails that dug into his throat.

"Thought I might find you in 'ere," Simon Frick hissed in Ned's ear. "You didn't really think you could run out on me, did you?"

"No, sir!" Ned gasped, as he struggled to breathe. "I can pay you, sir. I've got gold."

The long black fingernails sprang back, like a spider lifting its legs off its prey.

"Gold, you say?"

"Aye, sir. Right 'ere," Ned sputtered, as he dug into his shirt. He pulled out the pouch, whereupon Simon Frick reached over and grabbed it away from him.

"'At's right, Master Frick," Ned said nervously. "You go ahead and take a look. 'Tis real gold, surely enough to pay off my indenture and then some."

"Why, so there is." The sweep clicked his tongue against his rotted teeth as he greedily fingered the gold pieces in the bag. "There's more than double what I paid for you here."

Ned smiled uneasily. "Like I told you, sir, you can take out what I owes for my indenture and give me back the rest."

But the sweep made no move to hand over the gold. Instead he held up the bag and shook it next to his ear. "Now there's a pretty jingling, hey? Sweetest music I ever did hear. I'd be most interested in knowing how you came by it."

Ned gulped, as he tried to remember what Forrest had told him to say. "Found it," he lied. "Found it by a wagon near the mint."

The sweep's eyes narrowed. "Well, you're a clever lad to be keeping such a look out. Clever indeed."

"Thank you, sir," Ned said, his voice cracking.

"And well you should thank me, boy, for I've decided to keep this quiet and not take it up with the Constable."

"But, Master Frick, sir," Ned croaked. "The Constable don't need to know nothin', for that gold belongs to me."

But before he could get another word out, the sweep took the end of his broom and whacked Ned across the cheek with it, knocking him down.

"You sniveling vermin," Simon Frick snarled. "Nothing belongs to you. Not as long as you're indentured to me. You seem to forget that I own you, boy, and that means I own whatever crumb you may pick up on the street. Found this gold? A pretty story, but I've got a better one. You stole the gold and yer lying. So if I were you I'd forget you ever saw it. Get up now and come with me, for tomorrow you'll climb, bloody or not. And if you're lucky I won't be mentioning this business again."

"But my indenture," Ned protested, as he held his throbbing cheek. "You said yourself there was enough . . ."

"Who would ever believe you could pay it off yourself, you stupid boy?" the sweep replied. "'Tis your word against mine. And I say your indenture remains unpaid."

He reached into the pouch and plucked out a gold piece. "This one coin is as good as a rope around your neck," he whispered darkly. "If you ever try to run away from me again, I'll take this coin to the Constable and tell him how you stole the gold and spent it all, save for this last one that I found on you."

Ned shivered as the sweep put his thin, gray lips to the coin and bit. "'Twill just take my word and this one coin to put you in the cart to Tyburn," Simon Frick whispered. "And hung for the thief that you are."

"'Tis a lie," Ned whimpered. "A dirty lie."

"Downright filthy," the sweep laughed. "And there's the beauty of it, for no one will ever learn the truth." He pulled Ned up by the collar and dragged him to the door. "Come along now, Vermin," he hissed. "The others are waiting."

XXIV
LOVE AND COURAGE

That evening the Harpers' small cottage was filled with the spicy scent of cinnamon and hot plums coming from the crumble Mistress Harper had set on the hearthstone to cool. The freshly washed muslin curtain hung crisp and white from the cottage window. A cricket chirped from under a chair, and lark twigs crackled in the fire.

As Forrest bit into a hearty piece of bread, he seemed to notice everything around him as if he were seeing it for the last time. He noticed how kind his mother's round face was, how comforting her voice, as she shushed Beatrice in her cradle. He noticed his father's hands as he filled his pipe. The strength of those hands and the gentleness of them struck Forrest now. Even his sister Mary's smile seemed especially sweet to him.

After the meal, Forrest made a point of telling his mother how good her crumble tasted. He told Mary that she could play with his clay marbles if she liked.

And he even picked Beatrice up out of her cradle, though she smelled a bit ripe. He wanted to hold her close, to hold all of them to his heart and never let them go.

"You best fetch the prisoner her meal," his father called from his chair by the fire. "And take the rush lamp, for there is little moon tonight."

Forrest felt his heart begin to race once again at the thought of the darkness and the danger ahead of him. He kissed Beatrice's soft cheek before gently placing her back in her cradle.

Meanwhile, his mother packed the basket for Maddy. "I've added an extra piece of crumble," she said, and, seeing her husband's raised eyebrow she added, "She may be a Scot, but she is still a young girl all alone. The poor thing will have little to cheer her in these dark days."

Forrest avoided his mother's eyes and steadied his shaking hands as he reached for a long tin on the sideboard. He opened the box and pulled out a rush that had been rubbed with fat.

"Let me light it. Oh, do let me," Mary pleaded, taking the rush from his hand. Forrest watched as she held the tip of the rush to the fire until the fat began to sizzle and burn.

"Mind your skirts, Mary," the Ravenmaster warned.

Mary dutifully backed away from the hearth and handed her brother the lit rush. Forrest secured the iron clip onto the lamp and turned to leave.

"Have a care, dear," his mother warned, as she placed the basket in his free hand.

"And do not tarry long, for there is a chill in the air."

On any other night Forrest would have rushed out the door, hardly taking notice of his mother's fussing. But on this night he heard the concern in her voice and saw the love in her eyes. He wanted to tell her that it was not the chill in the air she need worry about, but something far more dangerous. For if things did not go well, he might never see any of them again.

Forrest felt his resolve begin to weaken. But when he thought of Maddy facing John Wilcox's axe, he knew he could not let her down.

She must have escaped by now, he reasoned. And if he failed to do his part, he would be placing her in the greatest danger. If someone else should discover that she was not in her cell, they would hunt her down. Every second counted, and he was desperate not to waste a single one. With his basket in one hand and his lamp in the other, he started out of the door.

"Have a care," he heard his mother call again, as he stepped outside. "And stay away from the moat."

Once outside, Forrest held up his lamp to light the way. A thick fog had swallowed up the path, except for the glow of a candle in a nearby cottage window.

As he walked, Forrest's knees grew weaker. The only sounds in the stillness of the night were of the small stones that crunched under his boots and seemed to whisper, "Hurry! Hurry! Hurry!" with each step. And soon his pounding heart drowned out the sound of his feet.

Where was Maddy now? Was she well on her way back to Scotland as planned? Did she escape, without being noticed? Would anyone suspect him?

By the time Forrest reached the Bloody Tower, his nerves were so frayed he feared he wouldn't be able to speak.

"Well, hallo, young Harper," Warder Marsh called from his post at the Tower's entrance. "What's happened to your father that he sends you in his place?"

"His back is ailing him," Forrest replied.

"'Tis the infernal dampness," Warder Marsh declared. "And the yeomen's curse it is, standing guard at the river's edge as we do."

"Aye, the dampness," Warder Thomas agreed with a frown. "The way it seeps right through your clothes and into your joints, as smooth as a thief in the night."

But the warder's face suddenly brightened. "Don't suppose the dampness bothers the ravens much," he said. "I hear from Henry Bothy your Tuck has learned quite a few good tricks."

Forrest nodded as he edged toward the Tower steps.

"What's your hurry, young Harper?" Warder Thomas smiled. " 'Tis only a prisoner's meal you've got to deliver."

"Why not show us what your raven can do?" Warder Marsh said jovially, as Forrest took the keys to Maddy's cell from the wall.

"Aye, sir, I'd be happy to," Forrest replied, "but I have work to do first." And he hurried into the Tower.

Up and up and up he climbed into the darkness, around and around the spiraling stairs. He reached out to brace himself on the cold, damp stones that encircled him. With each step he felt the grip of doubt and fear. His hands shook so badly, he nearly snuffed out the flame on his lamp.

When he finally reached the darkened cell, he held his breath and sighed with relief as he raised the light to the bars of the door. There in the corner lay a girl covered in Maddy's cape. She appeared so still that Forrest feared she was dead.

As quietly as he could, he fit the key into the lock

and pushed the door open. He stepped inside, and as he was about to set the basket on the table, the girl stirred. And as she sat up and turned around, Forrest found himself looking directly into a pair of piercing bluebell eyes.

"Maddy!" Forrest cried in horror. "Oh, Maddy!"

XXV
ONE MORE PROMISE

"What are you doing here?" Forrest gasped. "You should have left hours ago."

"No one came for me." Maddy began to sob. "One of the guards told me that new orders have come from the Constable, and I'm not to have any visitors."

Her voice broke off, and Forrest saw that her braid had come undone, and her hair fell below her shoulders, tangled and matted. The color had left her cheeks, and he ached when he saw that the circles had deepened beneath her eyes.

"The boat," Forrest whispered. "It will still be waiting for you at the King's Stairs tonight. If we can only get you there."

"But how?" she cried. "How am I to get out of this Tower and past the guards?"

"I don't know," Forrest admitted. And when he saw the frightened look in her eyes, he took her hands in his. "There must be a way."

She tried to smile, though her hands shook and her eyes welled with tears.

"I best leave now so as not to cause suspicion," Forrest said. "But I'll be back for you, Maddy. I promise I will get you out."

It wasn't until he was out on the darkened stairwell that Forrest realized the impossible promise he'd just made.

Forrest had lived within the Tower all his life. He knew just how strong and thick its walls were and how watchful its warders. He knew how merciless the Crown could be to those who dared to attempt an escape from the fortress's stony grip.

It was one thing for a boy to take part in a plan that was plotted by men of experience and cunning. But it was quite another for that same boy to attempt such a treacherous escape himself.

As he began the climb down the Tower's steps, Forrest was so distracted that he forgot the extra depth in the middle step. He fell forward, nearly losing his balance, and the basket flew from his hands. The clatter of his mother's wooden dish hitting the stone steps echoed up the stairwell as kidney pie and plum crumble splattered below.

How stupid could he be? He had forgotten to leave the supper with Maddy, and now it was ruined. Hot tears of shame stung his eyes. Who did he think he was that he could actually save her from the axe when he couldn't even deliver her a meal! But as he stared down at the mess, Forrest had an idea. Maddy still needed to eat. And surely the guards would understand that he needed to come back to the Tower with another meal for her. At least he'd have an excuse to return.

Just as he'd hoped, the warders shook their heads and laughed when he told them how he'd dropped the basket.

"I don't envy you having to tell your mother where her good cooking ended up," Warder Marsh joked, as Forrest rushed past him.

He dashed home and toward the shed, and he had just reached the door when he heard a familiar voice call his name.

"Ned!" Forrest whispered, and the two scurried into the shed together. "Why didn't you stay hidden? What were you doing out there?" The questions tumbled out as Tuck flew down from his rafter.

"Frick found me," Ned cried. And he told Forrest how the sweep had taken all the gold and threatened to tell the Constable if Ned told anyone.

"That dirty coward!" Forrest cried as he pounded the worktable with his fist.

Ned sighed. "He'd rather see me dead than free."

"But how did you escape?"

"Master Frick stopped in an alehouse near Mint Street. Me and the other climbing boys was to wait outside for 'im. They're so afeared of 'im they daren't disobey. But I slipped away as soon as 'Ee went in the door."

"You mustn't come to the shed anymore," Forrest told him. "And you mustn't come to the Tower, either. For he'll surely come back and look for you."

"What about Maddy?" Ned asked. " 'As she left the Tower yet?"

Forrest looked pained. "Everything went wrong. She's to have no visitors, so the plan to take her out in another's clothes was foiled. I told her I would go back to help, but I don't see how I can get her out now."

"Wot about me?" Ned offered. "Wot if I was to go back to the Bloody Tower with you. Me and Maddy could switch places. I can give her me clothes. It might work."

"But if it doesn't," Forrest whispered, "they'll hang you for sure."

Ned shrugged.

"You're willing to risk your life for her?" asked Forrest.

"She tried to save me with her ring. Besides, me life

ain't worth much with the sweep after me. Maybe at least one of us will live to be free."

"But won't Master Frick be looking for you?"

"Don't worry about him," Ned whispered. "He'll be in the alehouse for a while yet."

"Then we must leave now," Forrest said. "The warders are expecting me to return with another meal."

"And in case we meet up with the sweep on the way," Ned whispered ominously, "we jest might need this." He lifted the lid of the basket and dropped in the knife from the worktable.

Forrest's eyebrows shot up. "Do you really think we'll need it?"

"You never know."

Minutes later, the boys were on their way to the Bloody Tower. Ned held the lamp, while Forrest carried the basket. When a pair of regiment soldiers came up behind them, Ned was so startled he dropped the lamp and the rush went out.

They walked the rest of the way in darkness. The warder's torches flickered in the distance. Ned stumbled nervously over a broken cobblestone as Forrest jumped at the sudden hoot of an owl up in the eves of a portcullis. Together they both shivered in the mist that swirled about them.

As they approached the glowing torches at the entrance to the Bloody Tower, Ned grabbed hold of Forrest's sleeve.

"Back already?" Warder Thomas called on seeing Forrest approach.

"I'll wager your mother boxed your ears when you told her you needed another plate," Warder Marsh teased.

Forrest nodded as Ned rocked from one foot to the other.

"That step has caused many a broken bone," Warder Thomas said, shaking his head. "You're lucky you didn't crack your head open."

"Devil of a drop," Warder Marsh added.

Forrest held his breath as he watched the warder reach for the keys that hung from a ring at his waist.

"You'll need a light or you are sure to fall again," Warder Thomas told him.

Forrest took the rush lamp from Ned's trembling hand. "We do have a lamp, if you could give us a light."

The warder nodded as he took the lamp from Ned. "And I see you've found the little rat catcher. How is it you're all covered in soot?" He held the rush up to the lit torch in the iron hoop beside the Tower's door.

"Master Frick has taken him on as a climbing boy. Asked him to look at the chimney in my prisoner's cell," Forrest hurried to explain. "The flue's shut tight, and the room is frightfully cold."

"From rats to chimneys, hey?" the warder said, with a shake of his head.

Forrest wished he would just hand over the key. But Warder Marsh was in a talkative mood. "I hear the chimneys in the Warder's Hall were so . . ."

"Yes, well, we'd best fetch up this basket now," Forest interrupted him. "The prisoner hasn't yet had her sup," and he held out his hand for the key.

"Oh, aye, the key," Warder Marsh murmured. He was about to give it over when Warder Thomas brought his partizan up against Forrest's chest.

"Hang on there, lad, not so fast," Warder Thomas boomed. "What about your raven? I thought you said you were going to bring him 'round to show us some tricks."

"I'd forgotten you wanted to see him," Forrest said. "But I can bring him back after I deliver this food up. I promise I will."

Warder Thomas removed his weapon, and Warder Marsh was about to hand over the key when his dark eyes suddenly narrowed. He took a step forward and peered down at the basket in Forrest's hand.

"I hear tell your mother makes a fine kidney pie," he said, licking his lips. "It's been said your father's prisoners eat better than most at the Tower. Let's have a squint at what Mistress Harper has sent over tonight, hey?"

Forrest felt his knees begin to buckle as the warder motioned for him to open the basket.

XXVI
DON'T LET THEM HANG
ME IN A DRESS

"Truth be told," Forrest squeaked, as the warder waited, "Mother was feeling rather poorly today. Didn't cook a proper dish, just a crust and some drippings is all." He took a step back and bumped into Ned, nearly dropping the basket.

"About that raven of yours," Warder Thomas interrupted. "Just what kind of tricks can he do?"

"So many tricks," Forrest said. "You will hardly believe it. But I shouldn't want to spoil the surprise by telling you. I'll just fetch up this basket and when I'm through, I'll bring Tuck 'round and you can see for yourselves."

"Well, all right," Warder Thomas said. "But mind that step this time."

"Devil of a drop," Warder Marsh muttered again, as he handed Forrest the key.

Forrest and Ned hurried through the door and began the long climb up to Maddy's cell. When they reached her door, they found her on her knees.

"I prayed you'd come back, and you did," she whispered. "And Ned! Have you paid off the sweep?" she asked, turning to him. "Are you free?"

Ned shook his head.

"I lost the ring before I could give it to him," Forrest said sadly.

He watched her face cloud as she twisted a lock of her hair around her finger.

"But we must hurry now," Forrest said. "Ned has offered to trade places with you. He will give you his clothes."

"But how will *he* get out?" Maddy asked with concern.

Ned shrugged. "Don't be worryin' about me. Jest keep the cell door unlocked when you leave, and I'll manage to slip out the Tower door. I'm used to finding me way 'round this old fortress, though I ain't never done it in skirts."

"Nor I in breeches, but God willing, I'll do anything to get out of here," Maddy whispered.

"Then it's settled," Forrest said. "Now, give me your cape."

Maddy took off her cape and handed it to him. He held it up before her. "Both of you undress as quickly as you can," he commanded. "Hurry!"

Ned dropped his filthy jacket and trousers on the

floor while Maddy handed over a pile of two petticoats, a pair of pantaloons, a collar, cuffs, a shawl, a dress, stockings, and boots. "Hurry," Forrest whispered.

In a few moments, they were wearing each other's clothes. Forrest dropped the cape and took a look. Even dressed in Ned's rags Maddy still looked like a girl. And Ned looked no more convincing, for though the dress covered him well enough, his dirty face and soot-covered head gave him away.

Forrest turned to Maddy. "Your face is too clean," he said. "Ned, get some soot from the ash bucket."

Ned started across the room but almost tripped on his long skirts.

"You must lift them up as you walk," Maddy told him.

Ned made a face, but took her suggestion and returned with a handful of soot.

"Close your eyes," Forrest told Maddy, as he rubbed the soot into her cheeks and down her nose.

Meanwhile, Ned pulled a piece of charcoal from his pocket and began to work on her feet and ankles. Then the two boys stood back and took another look.

Ned placed his little blue cap on her head. He tried to stuff her long hair into it, but the cap was too small.

"It won't fit in," he finally said.

Forrest opened the basket and pulled out his knife.

Maddy's eyes widened at the sight of the blade. "What do you plan to do with that?" she gasped.

"Your hair," he whispered. "We must cut it off."

"Cut it off?" Maddy cried, as her hand flew up to her head.

"We must," Forrest tried to explain. "We have to pass by the sentries. If they have any reason to suspect you are not Ned, they'll stop you."

"Not my hair," Maddy exclaimed, as she twisted a long, golden strand around her finger. "I shall look . . . I shall look . . ."

"Alive," Ned finished her sentence for her. "You'll look alive."

"Ned is right," Forrest agreed. "If you want to keep your head on, we must take your hair off. There is no other way. It will grow back."

Maddy lowered her hands and squeezed her eyes shut tight. "All right, if you must, go ahead then and do it," she whispered.

Forrest reached out and grabbed a handful of her hair and began to cut. "Lucky for us we brought this," he said.

"Not many a lass would consider it good luck to lose her hair," Maddy replied weakly as her golden locks fell to the ground.

"Not many a girl would be trying to escape from the Tower of London," Ned reminded her.

When Forrest had finished, most of Maddy's beautiful hair lay on the stones at her feet. The short spikes of gold left on her head made for an uneven mess.

"You're beginning to look like me already," Ned told her as he picked up the fallen locks and threw them into the fire.

Maddy nervously brought her hand to her shorn head. "Oh, mercy," she whispered. "There's nothing left of it."

"There's enough to let you pass as Ned," Forrest told her. "And tonight that is all you shall need."

"I'm beginning to feel like him, too. Oh mercy, what's crawling on my skin?" Maddy cried.

"That's jest some lice," Ned said matter-of-factly. "Don't worry. You get used to 'um."

Forrest draped Maddy's cape around Ned's little shoulders and the climbing boy's tiny body seemed to be swimming in yards of green wool. His dirty face peered out of the cape's hood.

Maddy's transformation was now more convincing than Ned's. For with her hair cropped short and covered in soot, and with only Ned's rags to cover her, she looked as much like a boy as Ned.

"I feel awful." Maddy cringed and writhed in disgust. "I'm sure to catch the itch, and these rags have a powerful stink."

" 'Tis that stink that will save your life," Forrest told her, as he rushed to close the basket. "For the warders will remember smelling it on Ned as he came in." He turned to Ned.

"Count to one hundred and then come down the stairs and wait by the door," he told him. "I'll be back by then with Tuck. Wait for the right moment, and when the warders are looking away, you run out of the Tower as fast as you can."

But a look of horror had spread across Ned's filthy face.

"You never said nothin' about no countin'!" he cried. "I never learned me to count. I only know how to count to five."

"Just give us time to get to the shed. Then you can come down and wait by the door. You can do that, can't you?"

"Aye." Ned nodded.

"You won't have the lamp," Forrest reminded him. "Come down carefully. Keep your hand to the wall, and take care not to trip on the middle step."

"How will I know it's the middle?" Ned asked.

"You won't," Forrest told him, as he and Maddy headed for the door. "That is why you must take your time and be careful."

"Forrest," Ned called after him. "Promise me one thing."

"What's that?" Forrest asked.

"If they catch me," Ned whispered, "don't let them hang me in a dress."

XXVII
THE BEST NIGHT OR
THE WORST NIGHT

Seconds later, Forrest and Maddy climbed down the spiral staircase of the Bloody Tower. And as he placed his hand against the stairwell's cold, stone wall, Forrest couldn't help wondering if the next time he came up these steps it would be as a prisoner. He hoped and prayed that Maddy looked enough like Ned to fool the warders.

When they finally reached the bottom step, Forrest gave Maddy the basket to carry. "Keep your head down and your face turned away from the light," he whispered, his nerves jangling.

"I will," she whispered back.

Forrest could hear the tremor in her voice. "Everything depends on the next few minutes," he whispered. "Everything. Do you understand?"

Maddy nodded silently and made the sign of the cross.

"Are you ready?" he whispered.

In the glow of the rush lamp, he could see her

trusting eyes. Trusting him to do the right thing. Trusting him to save both their lives.

He took a deep breath, and, with his heart beating wildly in his chest, he led Maddy through the Tower's arched doorway and into the moonless night.

"Hold fast!" a deep voice ordered as Forrest and Maddy attempted to leave the Tower.

Forrest clutched Maddy's wrist with his free hand. Then he turned around and took a step toward the warder's light.

" 'Tis only us," he called.

"Thought you could sneak out without our noticing?" Warder Marsh demanded.

"You'd have to get up early in the day to pull one over on the likes of his Majesty's two best yeomen, hey, Joe?" Warder Thomas winked at his fellow warder.

Warder Marsh poked the basket in Maddy's hand with the tip of his partizan. "Any crumbs left?" he asked hopefully.

Forrest felt his knees begin to buckle. "No, Master Marsh. Sorry, sir," he said, as he tried taking the basket from Maddy, but she was clutching it so tightly he had to pry her fingers loose.

"That Scottish wench has a strong appetite, she has," Forrest croaked. "Finished her plate and asked for more."

"Hmm," Warder Marsh muttered. "I was hoping for a little morsel for myself."

"Yes, well, I best get home," Forrest stammered.

"Home and back," Warder Thomas reminded him. "For you are going to bring your raven for us to see now, aren't you?"

"Aye," Forrest replied. "You can depend upon it."

He led the way past the warders and into the shadows with Maddy following close behind. They were walking so fast the rush lamp once again went out.

"'Tis a good thing to have it out," Forrest whispered to Maddy. "The less light on us the better. I know the way."

As they walked along, Forrest looked up to the darkened battlements. He knew the watchmen were on guard. His eyes traveled across the shadows to the flickering lights of the sentries' torches that blazed before tower doorways. Forrest knew that any quick movement, any odd sound would give cause to sound the alarm. The entire fortress would be put on alert, and their fates would be sealed.

He struggled not to give in to the panic that was overtaking him. But how could he not panic? He had just helped a prisoner escape from her cell.

Forrest's head was dizzy with fear. They were out in the open. Anyone could spot them! Anyone could stop them! His teeth began to chatter uncontrollably, but he kept moving forward. Finally, after what seemed like hours, he saw the candlelight from the window of his family's cottage. He silently guided Maddy past it to the shed, where the two scurried inside for cover.

"You can use this," Forrest said, as he picked up an old blanket from a bench. He placed it around Maddy's shivering shoulders. Then he helped her to hide inside of an empty barrel, which he stacked with some wooden crates.

"You mustn't move from here until I return," he told her through his chattering teeth. He didn't want to tell her that he was worried Simon Frick could come looking for Ned.

"Must you go?" she whispered. "Can you not stay with me?"

"I must go back for Ned. I won't be gone long," he promised.

Forrest whistled for Tuck, and in moments, the raven landed on his shoulder.

"This could be the best night or the worst night of my life," Forrest whispered to his pet once they were outside the shed. "Maddy is not safe yet. None of us are. That is why I need your help."

The raven fluffed his tail feathers and snapped his beak closed. "Listen, now," Forrest commanded. "And if you are truly my friend, you'll do just as I say."

XXVIII
Can You Say "King George"?

When Forrest and Tuck finally reached the Bloody Tower's entrance, Forrest was alarmed to find that Warder Marsh was not at his post. If the warder had gone to check on his prisoner, Forrest knew all would be lost.

"Where is Master Marsh?" Forrest asked.

"He went to check on a noise," Warder Thomas motioned toward the shadows.

Forrest felt his blood run cold. What if Warder Marsh went up to Maddy's cell? He squinted into the shadows, frantic to see if Ned had come down yet. Meanwhile Warder Thomas was eager to see Tuck perform.

"Can he catch my coin, your raven?" he asked, pulling a halfpenny from his coat. He turned to Tuck. "Come now, if you can catch my coin your master shall have it for his pocket."

He threw the coin high in the air and Tuck flew from Forrest's shoulder, catching the coin in his beak.

Forrest held out his hand, and Tuck dropped the half-penny into it.

Glad as he was to see that Tuck was performing well, Forrest could barely concentrate for fear that Ned could run into Warder Marsh. But he let out a deep sigh of relief when he saw the warder appear from out of the shadows.

"You've come back in the nick of time, you have," Warder Thomas called, as Warder Marsh rushed forward to see the raven perform.

"Go on, then," Warder Marsh urged Forrest. "Show us another."

Forrest shifted anxiously from one foot to the other as he watched Warder Marsh position himself beside the Tower door. He needed to be clear of the area if Ned was to slip by unseen.

"If you would draw in closer," Forrest called, "You'd have a splendid view of the trick."

"I can see fine from here," the warder replied.

"Aye, but you cannot hear from there," Forrest tried again.

"Hear, you say?" Warder Marsh grumbled. "Wot's to hear?"

"What's to hear? What's to hear?" Forrest stalled as long as he could, trying to think of an answer. "Why, 'tis Tuck, of course," he finally said. "He speaks!"

"Oh, you've taught him to talk, have you?" Warder Marsh smiled.

"If you'll only move in closer, you shall hear him for yourself," Forrest replied.

To Forrest's great relief, both warders moved in closer.

"Let's hear this bird talk, then," Warder Thomas demanded. "I'll give you another halfpenny to hear him say 'King George.'"

Forrest rubbed his cheek against Tuck's soft feathers. "I know you've never done it before," he whispered to his pet. "But if there ever was a time you were thinking you might want to try to say a few words, this would be it. My very life may depend upon it."

Tuck blinked.

Forrest swallowed hard. "All right, then, Tuck, can you say 'King George?' Come on now. Say 'King George.'"

A long silence followed. Forrest stared hard at Tuck, willing him with all his might to talk. Then, as though the bird could understand the desperation of his beloved master, he puffed out his ruff, blinked hard, and squawked, "King George!"

Forrest stared in disbelief. Tuck had understood him! *You did it!* Forrest wanted to cry. *You did it!* But instead, he stroked Tuck's tail feathers as the raven puffed up proudly. "Jolly good, boy," Forrest said softly. "Jolly good."

"Why, 'twas clear as a bell," Warder Thomas marveled. "But can he say my name?"

"Say mine, say mine," Warder Marsh insisted.

The warders moved closer.

"There now, my friend Tuck," Warder Marsh cooed. "Can you say 'Joe Marsh?' Rolls off your tongue smooth as treacle, it does, 'Joe Marsh.' Come on there, Tuck, let's here you say 'Joe Marsh.'"

"How about Timothy Thomas?" Master Thomas wheedled. "There's a good bird. Say 'Timothy Thomas.'"

Meanwhile, as the warders coaxed and coddled Tuck, Forrest spotted a little green-clad figure, who silently slipped out of the Tower and disappeared into the darkness of night.

Forrest couldn't believe it. Ned and Maddy were out, and Forrest had kept his promise. Rather than run home like a frightened hare, he had stayed his ground like a man, like William the Conqueror! But his satisfaction was short-lived, as a familiar voice suddenly boomed from the doorway.

"Confound it, boy, did your mother not tell you to return straight home? 'Tis well past your bedtime." And without a moment of hesitation, his father took him by the ear and led him toward the Tower's entrance.

XXIX
Bedtime

"Father!" Forrest cried. "What are you doing here?"

"What indeed," Master Harper shot back. "I should be home resting my aching back is where I should be. But your mother wouldn't let me be for worrying about you. 'Tis almost nine o'clock. Did she not tell you to return straight home tonight?"

Forrest bit down on his lip. "Aye," he mumbled. "She did."

"Do not be too hard on the boy," Master Thomas interrupted. "For in truth, we encouraged him to come back and entertain us with his magnificent pet."

"We just heard the bird speak!" Warder Marsh exclaimed.

"Speak?" Master Harper repeated. He raised his lantern beside Tuck.

"The bird just said 'King George' clear as you please," Warder Thomas told him.

Master Harper's face softened as he turned to Forrest. "So, you've finally gotten him to speak. But I fear your mother won't be as impressed as I. Come along now, son, I think you've had enough excitement for one night. We best get home and to bed."

Master Harper bade the warders good night. But as he and Forrest walked back to the cottage, Forrest's mind was racing frantically. How could he go to bed? It was almost nine o'clock, and the Scots' rendezvous at the King's Stairs was at nine thirty. And where was Ned? Had he made it back to the shed? Or was he waiting in the shadows?

The one thing Forrest was certain of was that he could not go to bed.

"Father, might I sleep in the shed tonight?" Forrest pleaded. "I'm sure I could get Tuck to say more if I could only stay with him for a little longer."

"If he spoke tonight, he'll most likely do the same tomorrow," his father pointed out.

"Maybe, but 'tis just that I've been working so long with him, trying to get him to speak," Forrest persisted. "And now that he finally has, perhaps he will do more tonight."

"I can understand your desire to stay with him," his father said smiling, as the light from their cottage came into view. "But I daresay, your mother won't approve. She's sure to worry about your catching a chill or the pox or some such ill humors."

"I will sleep in the straw, and there's a blanket there besides. Oh, please, Father, do let me," Forrest begged.

"Well, all right." His father sighed, as they stopped before the shed door. "I'll speak to your mother. But if it turns too cold, you must come into the house."

"Thank you, Father," Forrest sighed with relief.

"I shall expect you up early as usual to do your chores," his father insisted, as he handed him the lantern.

"I will be, I will be," Forrest promised.

He watched as the Ravenmaster walked toward the cottage. Then he put his free hand on the wooden latch of the shed door and was about to lift it, when he heard his father call, "Oh, and Son?"

Forrest's hand froze on the latch. He lifted the lantern, but his father's figure had disappeared into the fog. "Yes, Father?" he called into the darkness.

"You've done a fine job with Tuck," his father answered. "Fine job, indeed."

"Thank you, Father," he called back. He held his breath as he listened for the sound of the cottage door opening and closing before he lifted the latch and stepped into the shed.

"Has Ned come back?" he asked Maddy, as he freed her from the barrel.

"No, no one has come," Maddy told him.

"I saw him leave the Bloody Tower," Forrest said. "He should have been here by now."

"There's a wicked fog tonight," Maddy said. "What if he's lost his way?"

"Or was stopped. . . ." Forrest whispered.

A long silence followed, for neither one of them wanted to imagine that.

XXX
DOWN THE KING'S STAIRS

Meanwhile, as the two friends hid in the darkness of the shed, there was another who sought to hide himself that night. On hearing footsteps behind him, Ned ducked into the shadows.

"Madeline! God be praised, you are out!" a deep voice whispered in Ned's ear, as a strong hand grabbed hold of him. "Come, there is little time to waste."

Ned recognized the long black robes of a priest. And as he struggled to free himself from the clergyman's hold, the hood of Maddy's cape fell from his head.

"What trickery is this?" the priest snarled, clasping Ned's throat with his large gloved hand. "Who are you? And what has become of the girl? Answer carefully, for your life depends upon it."

"I don't know nothin'," Ned croaked, as the priest's hand tightened around his throat.

"You lie," the priest growled. "I've been watching the Tower. The Ravenmaster's boy came out with a sweep, and now you. If you are not a friend to Madeline Stewart, what business brings you out this night wearing her cape?"

"But I am a friend to Maddy Stewart," gasped Ned.

"If that be true, I implore you to tell me all you know," the man whispered. "If you would see her away from this prison and alive, you must tell me her whereabouts so she can be saved."

"Me and 'er switched clothes so she could escape from the Tower. She's with Forrest, the Ravenmaster's boy, and they've gone to the Ravenmaster's shed."

The priest released his grip on Ned's throat. "Thanks be to God! If you speak the truth, then there still may be time to see her to safety. The guard has been detained. Can you and your friend get her to the King's Stairs at once?"

"Aye," Ned whispered.

"Then I must go there now and alert the boatman to wait. He's been paid handsomely for his services, but no amount of gold will keep him there long, as he fears the guards will spot his vessel. So hurry, boy, hurry!"

Right away, Ned lifted his skirts and ran.

When he reached the shed, Ned opened the creaky door, which startled Tuck who cawed sharply from above.

Maddy ducked, and Forrest raised his lantern to see who came. He sighed with relief when he saw Ned's dirty little face peering out from under Maddy's green cape.

"Ned!" Forrest cried. "You made it."

"Jest barely," Ned gasped, as he leaned against the worktable to catch his breath. "The fog is so thick I could hardly see, and I kept tripping over this bloody dress. And a man almost squeezed the air out of me, besides!"

"What happened?" Forrest asked.

Ned explained his surprise meeting with the priest and how he had gone ahead to the King's Stairs to wait for them.

" 'Tis my father's friend, Ewen MacDonald, disguised as a priest," Maddy whispered.

"Aye," Ned said, with a shake of his head. "But the boat is there now, and we got to hurry, for the guard has been detained, and the boatman won't be waitin' there long."

"Then let's be off," Forrest said, and the three stole out into the night.

The fog offered the perfect cover for the little group, though it made the going slow. They traveled close to the walls whenever they could. Forrest knew that one call or one shout from a soldier or sentry could bring every man in the fortress bearing down on them.

When they reached the Sally Port, he couldn't believe their luck, for the guard was still nowhere to be seen. *How had the priest detained him?* Forrest wondered. Maybe the Scots had paid him — or killed him. Forrest didn't stop to find out. The little drawbridge was all but swallowed up in the fog as he carefully led them over it.

When Forrest smelled the familiar strong scent of the river and heard the rippling of water, he felt his shoulders relaxing. They had made it. They had reached the wharf. But when he looked out over the river, he saw that there was no boat waiting.

"Oh Lord, have mercy, they have left without me!" Maddy cried out.

"We mustn't give up hope," Forrest told her. "They may be late because of the fog."

As the three made their way toward the King's Stairs, Tuck flew from Forrest's shoulder and circled above them.

"Shhh . . ." Forrest raised his finger to his lips. "Listen," he whispered. And as they did, they heard the sound of footsteps behind them. A long shadow appeared. It stoppped, then came closer.

"Maybe it's someone from the boat," Maddy whispered.

"Or a warder come to hunt us down," Forrest warned.

"Wot shall we do?" Ned whispered.

The children stopped breathing as the footsteps grew louder, and the shadowy figure edged closer. The clouds parted, and a patch of moonlight shone through the fog. Suddenly Forrest saw that it was not someone who had come to help them at all. For in that small sliver of light was the familiar stove-pipe hat and the corpselike grin glistening beneath it.

XXXI
DREE YER AIN WIERD

Forrest grabbed hold of Maddy's arm, and the three ran for their lives. But the sweep's long legs carried him so fast he was able to reach out and grab Maddy, pulling her from Forrest's grasp.

"Thought you could run out on me, little rat catcher?" the sweep hissed. "Well, I'll put an end to your running, I will."

"Let her go!" Ned demanded. He pulled the cape's hood from his head. "'Tis me you want, not her."

"Wot's this?" Simon Frick muttered, as he looked from Maddy to Ned. "Wot goes 'ere? Is that you, Vermin, dressed in skirts? And who might you be?" he hissed in Maddy's ears, giving her a rough shake.

"Take your dirty hands off me," Maddy cried, as she struggled to get free.

"Ah, a Scottish brogue, is it?" Simon Frick whispered.

"Leave the girl be, and I'll go with you," offered Ned, his voice cracking with fear.

Forrest shivered at the sight of Simon Frick's thin lips curling into another smile.

"A generous offer," the sweep wheezed. "But have you really learned your lesson?"

"I won't run away again, I swear," Ned cried.

"Perhaps if you were to lose an eye, or maybe your nose, that might prevent you from straying," the sweep wheezed, as he held up his dagger.

"If you harm him in any way, I shall tell my father, and he will have the Constable arrest you," Forrest threatened.

The sweep's gray face twisted into a smile. "Oh, yes, your father and the Constable," he murmured. "Capital idea. Do call them, Bird Boy. But I shouldn't think they'd be as interested in the likes of this little vermin's fate." He lifted Ned with one hand and shook him. "No, I daresay they wouldn't find his bony carcass all that interesting. Though they might pause to wonder why he is dressed in this lovely green frock. That might capture their attention, that and this little Scottish wench here, waiting down by the river. Would it be a boat you'd be waiting for, Miss?"

Forrest felt his mouth go dry. " 'Tis not your business," he said.

"Ah yes, business." The sweep grinned. "I've heard tell treason is a dangerous business, but then I wouldn't know, would I? No, I've me own business to attend to now, so I'll leave you to yours. And I promise you this, Bird Boy, if you dare to rub your nose in my business again, I shall take an interest in yours. Yes, the Constable of the Tower would be most interested in your whereabouts this night, I reckon." He held up his dagger.

"Let's you and me take that walk now, Vermin," Simon Frick whispered into Ned's ear, as the knife's blade grazed his throat. "Just a short walk is all we shall need."

Forrest and Maddy froze, as they watched the stooped figure pushing Ned forward, the ends of the green cape trailing in the mud. Forrest knew that if he tried to rush the sweep, the dagger in his hand could easily pierce Ned's neck. But he couldn't just let them walk away. He couldn't let the sweep hurt Ned. He gave a sharp whistle, and a sudden flapping of wings sounded overhead.

"Wot's that, then?" Simon Frick hissed, as Tuck swooped down low and grazed the top of his hat. The sweep cursed and tried waving Tuck away with his dagger, but the raven was able to dodge him. He swooped down again, and this time he lifted the sweep's hat from his head and dropped it over the rank, murky water.

"Blasted raven!" Simon Frick shouted, as he shoved Ned along. "I'll take your bloody nose off right now!"

He raised his dagger and carefully aimed at Ned's face when Tuck flew in low and laid a mighty peck at the back of the sweep's neck.

Simon Frick cried out in surprise as he spun around to shoo away the bird, but he tripped over Ned's cape. He fell face forward onto his dagger, gasping and choking and clutching his breast as he writhed in pain. His mouth opened, his eyes rolled back, and he gave three rasping breaths. Then he fell silent.

The children stared wide-eyed at the motionless figure on the ground.

"Do you think he's dead?" Maddy whispered.

"I don't know," Ned said.

"But if he is not," Forrest said, "he's sure to come after us. Quick! Let's run!"

Forrest could barely make out the river as they raced toward the King's Stairs. Were those footsteps behind them or just the sounds of their own feet?

They dared not stop and find out. It wasn't until they reached the bottom step that they saw the boat gliding toward them through the fog.

"They're here!" Maddy whispered breathlessly. "They're here!"

Forrest could see Ewen MacDonald sitting beside a boatman, who manned the oars. Forrest and Ned rushed to help Maddy into the boat.

"God be praised," Ewen MacDonald said, as she fell into his arms. Then he turned to Forrest. "Were you followed?"

"Yes," Forrest whispered, "but only by one, and he tripped and fell onto his dagger. I think he is dead."

"The Lord looks after the innocent," MacDonald said. "And if you two need sheltering, come aboard. We're indebted to you both after what you've risked tonight. We can promise you safe passage once we're out of English waters."

"Oh, yes, do come with us," Maddy pleaded. "You can both leave this dreadful place forever."

Ned nodded eagerly, but Forrest was caught off guard.

"Forever?" Forrest whispered under his breath. He understood that if he were to leave now, it would mark him as guilty and he could never return.

"We've always dreamed of leaving," Ned whispered. "Now our dream of going out in the world to have real adventures has come true."

"Best hurry if you're coming, lads," the boatman called.

Ned's enthusiasm gave Forrest all the encouragement he needed to grab hold of the boat. He was about to climb in when he turned his head toward the Tower for one last look. The fog was so thick, he couldn't make it out. And as he stared into the swirling mist, his thoughts suddenly turned to his family. How heartsick would his mother be if he were to disappear forever? Who would help his father with the ravens? Who would make Mary laugh by turning Bea into a pirate? And would little Bea even remember that she had had a big brother? How was he to leave them all forever? At that moment, he knew that it wasn't his destiny to go but rather to stay!

"You go on without me," he said, letting go of the boat.

"Wot are you talking about?" Ned cried.

"I can't go," Forrest tried to explain. "This is my home. My family is here. My life is here. My father expects me to be Ravenmaster one day. And I think I shall be a good one." Then he turned to Maddy. "You were right. It does take courage to face your destiny."

"You always had that courage," Maddy said, reaching out for his hand. "You two are the bravest boys I know. How can I ever thank you for all you've done for me?"

"I don't know what to say," Ned said, turning to Forrest. "You've been the best of friends to me." Ned looked anxiously at the boat. "I always hoped you and me and Tuck would never part."

Forrest felt his heart breaking at the thought of never seeing Ned again.

"Maybe we won't have to," Forrest whispered as he pulled the spyglass off his neck and held it out to his friend. "You take it," he said. "You can use it to find me no matter where you go. Just point it in the direction of the Tower, and Tuck and I will be thinking of you. Just look through it in the special way we always do, and you'll see us both. I promise you will."

"Are you sure you want me to have it?" Ned cried, clutching the spyglass to his heart.

"I'm sure."

"I won't ever forget you," Ned whispered.

"And I won't forget you. For I doubt I could forget how dreadful you look in that dress."

They both smiled as they fought to hold back their tears, and Ned curtsied. Then the Rebel Scot offered Ned a hand and helped him into the boat.

"Are you coming, boy?" the boatman asked, nodding toward Forrest.

"No," Forrest told him. "I live here."

"Then hurry, lad, and give us a push," the boatman answered. And because his arms were strong enough and because his heart was big enough, Forrest was able to give them just the push they needed to send their boat into the river, out of harm's way, and out of his life forever.

Later that night, as Tuck folded his wings high up on a rafter in the shed, Forrest sank down into the straw below him. But he couldn't settle his mind into a peaceful sleep. As happy as he was for his friends who were safely sailing to freedom, he was also overwhelmed with the sorrow of his loss, for he knew he would never see them again.

"It's just you and me now, Tuck," he whispered softly in the dark. The raven, hearing his name, murmured from above, as he fluffed out his feathers. And then, as if he understood all that was in his master's heart, Tuck rustled through his hoard of treasures. Seconds later, Forrest felt a small, hard object hit him on the head.

"Giving me a present, are you?" he asked.

Though it was too dark to see, he managed to search through the straw until his fingers clasped around the hard, smooth band. And in the tiny ray of moonlight that shone through a crack in the shed's door, he saw the red of the stone.

With his heart beating wildly, Forrest fingered the

inside of the band. He needed no light to read the words inscribed there.

"*Dree yer ain wierd,*" he whispered aloud, as he clutched the ring tightly. "Face your destiny." And he smiled, for he understood that he had found the courage to do just that.

XXXII
He Had a Shifty Look

The next morning, when Forrest Harper reported to the sentries at the Bloody Tower that his prisoner was not in her cell, the entire fortress was thrown into an uproar. The Tower's drawbridges were instantly raised and the Constable ordered a full inspection. Soldiers and warders alike fanned out over ramparts, up and down stairways, and along battlement walls.

It was then that the bloodied body of Simon Frick was discovered beside the river. Forrest and his father were both questioned and released. Warders Thomas and Marsh were questioned as well. They reported that Simon Frick had come looking for Ned that night. He had insisted on going up to look for him in the Tower, even after both warders had told him the boy had left.

"He had a shifty look to him," Warder Marsh said of the sweep. "A most untrustworthy figure, I'd say."

The fact that Simon Frick's pockets were filled with gold led the King's investigators to surmise that he was paid to help the prisoner escape and had fallen out with the Scots, whereupon they killed him with his own dagger. With Frick dead, the Crown was satisfied, and the case was closed.

The Tower seemed especially dark and dreary to Forrest as he went about his chores in the days and weeks that followed. For now when he drew battles on the shed wall, he had no one to share them with, and they seemed less exciting than his own life had been. When he prepared the ravens' meals, he prepared them alone. And when he climbed the Bloody Tower's steps to tend to his father's new prisoner, an old, silent duke, he heard no more stories about a sun-filled Glen and the buttercups that grew there.

Foggy nights found Forrest thinking of Ned and their final good-bye beside the river's edge. And when the moon was full, it was Maddy's face he saw shining down upon him.

But Forrest's loneliness began to lessen as time went on. With his newfound confidence, he began to see things differently. The bullies began to look more like ordinary boys. And slowly, without his even noticing at first, the Tower walls began to take on a different look as well. They didn't seem quite as high to him as they once had.

And then one day, Forrest stopped wishing to live in the world beyond those ancient walls. And instead, he made himself a good life within them. But he kept the memory of the adventure he'd had close to his heart, and he often relived it in his mind. And as he never left the fortress to have the adventures he'd once dreamed of, he clung to the hope that someone else had. He would close his eyes and call him up in his mind, as he whispered to the raven at his side.

"I see him, Tuck. He's running on a beach beside the ocean. His blue cap is pulled over his brow. The sun is blazing so bright. He's got the spyglass to his eye, and what's that he sees? Bless my soul, if it isn't a pirate ship coming round the cove!"

And, in that way, one more adventure would be born and one more journey taken, there in the middle of all that mortar and stone.

Epilogue:
A Secret from Long Ago

Days passed and weeks flew by and, in the blink of a raven's eye, thirty springs had come and gone. The bluebells continued to bloom and wither beside the Chapel Royal's door. As fledglings spread their wings and boys grew into men, the Tower's stony walls stood as high and unyielding as ever.

It was a cloud-covered day in March that found the Tower's Ravenmaster standing within those walls.

"Hear that, Tuck?" he whispered to the old raven, who was perched on his shoulder. "They're raising the gates. Company coming!"

The bird's eyes, dull black pearls, seemed to brighten as he cocked his head. Together the two watched as a number of new prisoners were led over the drawbridge. Workmen and tradesmen with their carts and wagons followed.

But it was one small figure in this last group who caught the Ravenmaster's attention. He was but a wisp of a boy, so wafer thin he looked as if he might blow away in the strong March wind. The Ravenmaster's dark eyebrows shot up at the sight of the scamp's ragged clothes and dirty little face. And suddenly the memory of another boy flooded his mind.

"Are you the Ravenmaster?" the boy called. "Ravenmaster Forrest Harper?"

Startled, the Ravenmaster blinked and looked down to see the poor waif standing before him.

"Aye," he answered. "I am he."

"Then this is for you," the boy said, holding out a package wrapped in brown paper.

"For me? But who sent it, lad?"

"Ain't me business to know," said the boy with a shrug. "I just deliver packages from the wharf 'round the city. Don't know who they come from nor what they be." He stood waiting hopefully.

"Yes, all right," muttered the Ravenmaster, as he dug into his pocket. He pulled out a penny and threw it to the boy.

"Is that one of the Tower's ravens?" the boy asked, motioning to the bird on the man's shoulder.

"One of the oldest," the Ravenmaster told him.

"Does he do tricks?"

"Tricks?" The Ravenmaster smiled. "He could teach you a few, I daresay."

He reached into his pocket for another coin and

threw it high into the air. The raven flew after it and caught it in his beak.

"Hold out your hand, lad," the Ravenmaster ordered.

The boy did as he was told, and the raven dropped the penny into his palm.

As the boy walked away, the Ravenmaster smiled at the bird on his shoulder. "Not bad for a couple of old fellows, hey, boy?"

The raven murmured softly and nuzzled his neck.

Then the two headed home to a cottage beside the moat. The raven flew to the roof as the man went up to the door. No sooner had he stepped inside than his rosy-faced daughter raced up to meet him. He smiled as he lifted the black velvet hat from his head and placed it into her small waiting hands.

"How goes it with you, sir?" his wife asked, as she offered to take his coat.

"As it should, my love, as it should," the Ravenmaster replied. "For no sooner am I in the door than our Maddy, here, meets me and, in two shakes of a duck's whisker, she has my bonnet ready to put away. Fine job, my girl, fine job."

The little girl grinned as she placed the large hat on the shelf beside the door. "Father, what have you brought us?" she asked, as she hurried back to his side.

The Ravenmaster looked down at the small package under his arm and shook his head. "Oh this," he said. "A boy from the docks delivered it today. In truth, I do not know what it is."

He took his seat by the fire while his wife went back to rolling out her oatcakes. And as his young daughter looked on, the Ravenmaster untied the string from the package and pulled open the brown paper.

"What is it, Father?" his daughter asked.

"'Tis a spyglass," the Ravenmaster whispered, as he pulled it out of its old leather case. "A very old spyglass."

"But who would send such a thing?" his daughter wondered aloud. "Is there no message come with it?"

It was then that the Ravenmaster noticed the letter tucked into the brown wrapping paper. And with a trembling hand he picked it up and read aloud:

To Ravenmaster Forrest Harper
The Tower of London

Dear Forrest,

It has been many years and a lifetime ago since last we spoke. I have followed my dreams and searched for a place that is as free of chimneys and rats as any

A SECRET FROM LONG AGO

I know. And so the sea has become me home. With the Stewarts' aid, I was able to secure work on a whaling ship, and have since sailed 'round the world these many years past.

When last I heard, the Stewarts were living in the colonies. Maddy was well and happy. Once long ago, you loaned me a spyglass. Do you recall? Because of you, I was able to see further than I had ever dreamed. I return it now with my thanks, which are much overdue. If you direct the glass south, toward the Mediterranean Sea, you will be looking in the direction of an old friend who has not forgotten the times we spent together and the secret we share.

In gratitude, Yours, Ned White,
Captain in His Majesty's Royal Navy

"But Father," little Maddy pestered, as she looked through the old brass spyglass. "It is so cloudy, I cannot see anything through it."

"You have to look in a special way," the Ravenmaster told her. As he guided his hand over hers, his fingers grazed the ruby ring she wore on her thumb. "You have to *really* look."

She shrugged and tried again but quickly lowered

213

the glass. "And, Father, how did this sea captain know of me and that I was happy?"

A smile came upon her father's face then, and a faraway look filled his eyes.

"'Tis a secret, my love," the Ravenmaster whispered, hugging her to him. "A secret from long ago."

        ❧   ❧   ❧

The Tower Through Time

The Tower's Beginning

In the winter of 1066, William the Conqueror began work on his palace-stronghold overlooking the city of London. The first stone tower to be built was the White Tower. Over the next two hundred and fifty years, Britain's kings enlarged the fortress to include additional towers, a mint, a jewel house, an armory, a record's office, a lodgings, a barracks, a zoo, and a prison.

The Tower Zoo

During his reign, Henry III was given an elephant by the king of France, three leopards by the emperor of Germany, and a polar bear by the king of Norway. King Henry decided to keep his growing menagerie at the Tower. This was the start of the Tower's zoo.

Some Famous People at the Tower

Thousands of prisoners passed through the Tower over the centuries. Two of the Tower's youngest prisoners were the sons of King Edward IV. They were brought to the Tower in 1483 following their father's death. The boys remained in the Tower for several months and were never seen alive after that. No one knows for sure how they met their end, but rumors spread that their uncle Richard, who wanted the Crown for himself, had them murdered in the Garden Tower, which was thereafter called the Bloody Tower.

In the year 1554, the future Queen Elizabeth I was held prisoner in the Bell Tower when she was just twenty years old. Her stay was short, and, once on the throne herself, Queen Elizabeth did not hesitate to use the Tower to punish those who displeased her.

Sir Walter Raleigh was one of those unlucky enough to fall out of favor with the crown, and was locked in the Bloody Tower for thirteen years. He spent his time there writing his book, *The History of the World*, which contained one million words!

In 1668, a soon-to-be famous American was held prisoner in the Tower. A young William Penn, the Quaker who would later become the founder of Pennsylvania, landed in a Tower cell after publishing a pamphlet that attacked the Crown's religious beliefs. He was held for seven months before his father was able to maneuver his release.

TORTURE

Torture was used at the Tower to force prisoners to confess. There were various methods of torture used. The Rack was used to stretch a prisoners' joints. The Scavenger's Daughter did the opposite by squeezing a prisoner's body parts in a painful contortion. A tiny torture cell, called Little Ease, was used to hold prisoners in a painful contortion for long hours. Manacles were used to hang prisoners from their wrists.

By the 1700s, torture was no longer in use at the Tower. But the cold, damp site of the fortress, sitting so close to the Thames River, coupled with the rats and the filth of the times, often led to a tortured existence for the prisoners kept there.

TOWER EXECUTIONS

Some of Britain's most famous executions took place at the Tower. King Henry VIII had two of his six wives executed on Tower Green. They were Ann Boleyn, who was executed in May 1536, and Catherine Howard, who was executed in February 1542. Both were in their early twenties when they lost their heads. Lady Jane Grey also lost her head. She was just sixteen years old and had reigned as Queen of England for only nine days. Thomas Cromwell, Henry VIII's chief minister, was executed at the Tower in 1540.

THE MIGHTY FORTRESS

It was not an easy thing to escape from the Tower. The buildings proved impossible to break through. In some places, walls were fifteen feet thick. To enter the fortress from land, three draw-bridges had to be crossed.

The many gates and portcullises (heavy wooden drop gates hung in the arches) that were manned by guards could be lowered at the first sound of an alarm. Murder holes over the arches allowed for the spilling of molten lead or boiling water. Bailey walls rose up forty feet and higher to meet the battlements. Outer walls were pierced with arrow slits to defend the fortress from attack across the moat.

The moat offered a strong deterrent. Not many dared to swim through the thick raw sewage. The muck and slime not only carried disease but also was difficult to swim through.

Only those brave and strong dared to attempt an escape from such a mighty prison.

Great Escapes

Though the characters in *The Ravenmaster's Secret* were not real, their plan to get Maddy out of the Tower was based on a number of real escapes.

The first recorded successful escape from the Tower of London was by Bishop Ranulf Flambard in 1101. He had a wine jug with a hidden rope delivered to his cell. With his rope, Flambard was able to lower himself from an uppermost window in the White Tower and escape to freedom.

Over the centuries a number of determined prisoners followed in Flambard's footsteps, and, with a combination of wits, luck, and determination, were able to make their escapes.

Some, like Flambard, slid down ropes, while others hid in workmen's carts and were wheeled out of the Tower. A few were able to brave the moat and swim to freedom. Still others disguised themselves and actually walked out of the Tower! One such prisoner was William, Fifth Earl of Nithsdale (a Scottish noble and Jacobite). It was his young wife, Winifred, who masterminded his escape in 1716. Providing her husband with a wig, dress, and shawl, Lady Nithsdale was able to walk her husband out of the Tower dressed as her maid!

If you are interested in more facts about Tower escapes, you can read about them on the Tower of London's Web site. For the first time in history, the Tower's Record Office is making the prison records public.

THE TOWER TODAY

The Tower's use has changed over the centuries. Royalty no longer lives there. Money is no longer minted on the Tower grounds. The lions and elephants are gone, since the zoo was closed in 1834. And the last prisoner to be held at the Tower was during World War II.

Today millions of people from all over the world visit the Tower, not as prisoners, but as tourists! The Yeoman Warders still live at the fortress with their families, but instead of prison guards, they now serve as tour guides.

You can learn more interesting facts about the Tower's past and present on the Web site or in any number of books on the Tower's history. If you visit the Tower, be sure to stop by the ravens' cages for a visit with the magnificent birds.

Glossary

English Words

BALLADEER: the singer of a narrative poem-song

BREECHES: trousers

BROADSWORD: a straight, flat sword, usually with a basket hilt

CHAMBER POT: a night pot used as a toilet in the days before indoor plumbing

CHEEKY: forward manner; rude

COLLAR DAY: hanging day

FLEDGLING: a young bird that is about to fly

FLITCH: ham

GINGER BISCUIT: ginger cookie

MOAT: water that surrounds a fortress for protection

MURDER HOLE: a hole located above an entranceway in a gatehouse, which can be used for dropping missiles or molten liquids on uninvited enemies

NAUGHT: none

PORTCULLIS: a strong arched iron gate that prevents passage into a fortified place

RUFF: stiff collar or neck feathers

RUSH LAMP: lamp made from a rush plant soaked in fat

SCAFFOLD: a platform on which a criminal is executed by hanging or beheading

SHIFT: a loose-fitting dress

TURRET: a small ornamental tower

TYBURN JIG: the sharp dance-like movements of a hangman's body as the noose tightens around his neck.

Tyburn was where London's lower criminals were executed.

WENCH: girl or young woman

YEOMAN WARDER: attendant or guard in a royal or noble household.

SCOTTISH WORDS

BIDE AWEE: wait a bit

BONNIE: fair, pretty

BONNIE PRINCE CHARLIE: the fair-looking heir to the Scottish throne

CLAN: connected group of families

DIRK: highland dagger

DREE YIER AIN WIERD: face your destiny

GLEN: valley

GAELIC: any of the Celtic languages of Ireland, Scotland, or the Isle of Man

HEATHER: heath plant

JACOBITE: follower of Stuart line to English throne

KILT: a plaid pleated skirt. The type of plaid signifies clan membership.

LOCH: lake

ROWAN: European mountain ash. A tree with red berries

SECOND SIGHT: to be able to see the future

TATTIE-BOGLE: scarecrow

WEE: small

WEE HOOLIT: small baby owl

WHEEN O'BLETHERS: a pack of nonsense

BIBLIOGRAPHY

The following books were consulted for the research for *The Ravenmaster's Secret*.

ABBOT, G. THE BEEFEATERS OF THE TOWER OF LONDON. LANCASHIRE, UK: HENDON PUBLISHING CO. LTD., 1985.

ABBOT, G. GREAT ESCAPES FROM THE TOWER OF LONDON. LANCASHIRE, UK: HENDON PUBLISHING CO. LTD., 1982.

BOTSFORD, JAY BARRETT. *ENGLISH SOCIETY IN THE EIGHTEENTH CENTURY*. NEW YORK: MACMILLAN CO., 1924.

BRANDER, MICHAEL. *THE SCOTTISH HIGHLANDERS AND THEIR REGIMENTS*. NEW YORK: BARNES AND NOBLE INC., 1974.

BRIGGS, ASA. *A SOCIAL HISTORY OF ENGLAND*. NEW YORK: VIKING PRESS, 1983.

HAMMOND, PETER. *DISCOVERING THE TOWER OF LONDON*. LEICESTERSHIRE, UK: LADYBIRD BOOKS, 1987.

HARRISON, BRIAN. *A TUDOR JOURNAL: THE DIARY OF A PRIEST IN THE TOWER*. LONDON: ST. PAUL'S PUBLISHING, 1988.

HEINRICH, BERNARD. *MIND OF THE RAVEN*. NEW YORK: CLIFF STREET BOOKS, AN IMPRINT OF HARPERCOLLINS, 1999.

HIBBERT, CHRISTOPHER. *The Tower of London.* London: The Reader's Digest Association Ltd., 1971.

KEAN, MARY. *Scottish-English English-Scottish.* London: Abson Books, 1972.

LAPPER, IVAN AND GEOFFREY PARNELL. *Landmarks in History: The Tower of London.* UK: Osprey Publishing, 2000.

LIVINGSTONE, SHEILA. *Scottish Customs.* New York: Barnes and Noble Inc., 1996.

PARNELL, GEOFFREY. *The Tower of London Past and Present.* Gloucestershire, UK: Sutton Publishing, 1998.

POOL, DANIEL. *What Jane Austen Ate and Charles Dickens Knew.* New York: Touchstone, 1993.

PORTER, ROY. *English Society in the Eighteenth Century.* London: Penguin Books, 1983.

WILLIAMSON, AUDREY. *The Mystery of the Princes.* Chicago: Academy Chicago Publisher, 1992.

WILSON, DEREK. *The Tower of London: A Thousand Years.* London: Hamish Hamilton Ltd., 1978.

FOR MORE ABOUT THE BOOK

GO TO

www.scholastic.com

for

The Ravenmaster's Secret

Teaching Guide

Perfect for students, parents, and teachers!